Lift high his royal banner,
It must not suffer loss:
From victory unto victory His army shall He lead,
Till every foe is vanquished, and Christ is Lord indeed.

—STAND UP, STAND UP FOR JESUS

Thy KINGDOM Come: The Promise of the King

All Scripture passages in this book are taken from the Authorized King James Version, any deviations are not intentional.

Published by DayStar Publishing
P.O. Box 464
Miamitown, Ohio 45041

ISBN: 9781890120887
LOCN: 2013933328

Cover and maps were created by Second Mile Media.
http://www.secondmilemedia.org/

Thy KINGDOM Come
SCHWORERTKC

Thy KINGDOM Come

The Promise of the King

By Rick Schworer

Note to reader: while the overall story of the kingdom of heaven is true, this is a work of fiction based upon the author's interpretation of the Bible and history. Additionally this is not an attempt to breathe life into the Scriptures but rather to demonstrate that the Bible is the most amazing book ever written. May God bless you while you study these things out for yourself.

Other than the cover and maps, all images are public domain and are used for their classical and timeless value; they are not necessarily the author's impression of what these characters or events appeared as.

This book tells the story of some amazing leaders such as Moses and Joshua, and is dedicated to another great one in today's battle for the kingdom of God:

Pastor Rick DeMichele

Introduction

I hope you enjoy this dramatized retelling of the story of the kingdom of heaven.

This is not the story of the whole Bible. This is not the story of the kingdom of God; that's a spiritual kingdom based on spiritual warfare. This story, in its essence, is not even the story of redemption that we all know and love, though that plays a major part. This is the story of a physical and earthly kingdom that by and large has been won and lost by physical and earthly warfare.

This story is about flawed human beings throughout history that God used in mighty ways. These individuals all had their highs and lows; they all had times of failure and valor. But just as this story is about people, it's also about the hope they all possessed.

This is a story on authority. This story is about a King and a kingdom that primarily pertains to one of the bloodiest chunks of ground the world has ever known: Israel.

This is the story of a promise, which is as of yet unfulfilled and was given roughly six thousand years ago to two guilty people who stood trembling before

God; a promise about the day in which the serpent's head would be bruised.

That promise has meant different things to different people throughout history, and it's had a few other promises come along with it: namely, three hundred thousand square miles of land in the Middle East.

Between God and Satan lies the will of a group of people who will either accept the kingdom and its requirements or suffer the consequences. Voyage through time as Satan attempts to stop or stall the fulfillment of the Garden Promise and his own eternal reckoning.

Rest assured, the King will come and will bring with him the final consummation of the kingdom, and when he does it will be a kingdom of peace. Until that day expect war and mayhem, religion and faith, betrayal and treachery. Until his kingdom comes and his will is done on Earth as it is in Heaven, we live under a curse.

Even so, come, Lord Jesus.

TABLE OF CONTENTS

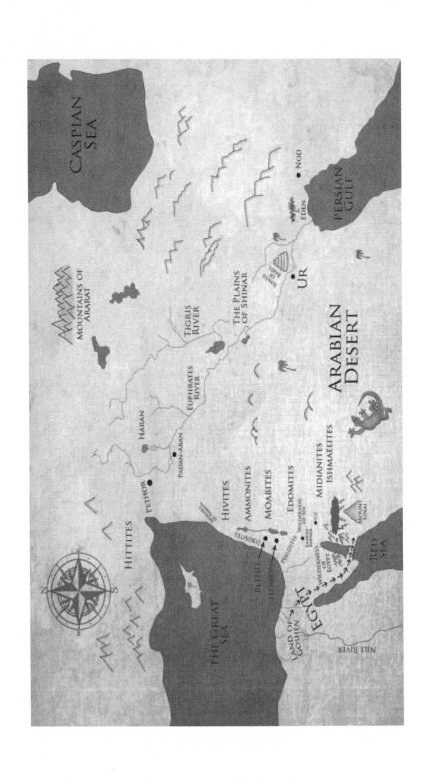

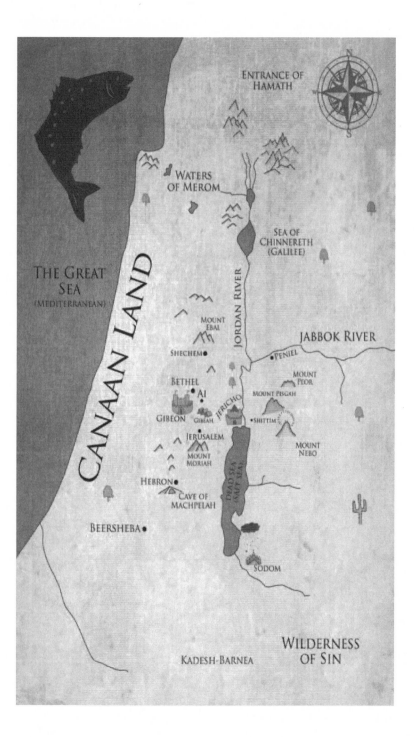

Chapter One

"When the morning stars sang together, and all the
sons of God shouted for joy?"
Job 38:7

Not Long Before Adam: Outer Space

In the beginning God created the heaven and the earth. Streaking comets lighted the emptiness of space as stars erupted from nowhere. Innumerable greenish-blue gasses whirled and pulsed, spinning like tops through the darkness. Planets materialized, some in completeness while others had their parts suspended in space and placed together by unseen hands. Giant blue and red orbs throbbed with light as they appeared from nothingness, changing sizes rapidly from smaller to larger and back again and then hurtling through space to parts unknown.

The manifold majesty of Jehovah was on full display for the supernatural beings that hovered and gazed. "Give glory to the God of creation!" Lucifer shouted, and in a triumph of glory the morning stars sang together and all the sons of God shouted for joy.

"Hallelujah to the LORD of Heaven and Earth!"

"Praise him, praise him, praise him!"

Having been created only moments before and led by the beautiful and musical Lucifer, the angelic host praised the Almighty for many years after the creation.

And when the music and praise finally stopped, there was silence.

"Lucifer, thou art the anointed cherub that covereth; and I have set thee so," God said. "With your beauty you will reflect my glory back upon me."

Millions of eyes turned and looked upon the golden body of Lucifer that was speckled with precious stones and jewels.

"With the workmanship of thy tabrets and of thy pipes you will lead my host in praise."

Lucifer bowed in humility.

"Lastly," the LORD said, "it will be your duty to care for the Earth; with your wisdom you will be responsible for dressing and keeping Eden, the Garden of God."

Lucifer spoke. "Thank-you, LORD God Almighty, I am honored to serve you however you wish."

Time came and went and it was over time that three particular beings were elevated above the others: Michael, for his strength and power. Gabriel, for his wisdom and eloquence. And of course Lucifer, who for all intents and purposes was second to God himself. He was the fifth cherub that covered the throne of God and had the greatest honor of all: leading the worship.

It was on this particular day that Lucifer was doing just that, preparing others in preparation for a great upcoming ceremony for the LORD. He was interrupted, however, by Gabriel, who lighted down next to him.

"Lucifer," Gabriel said, "the LORD requests your presence at the throne."

Lucifer turned in his throne and shifted slightly. "Very well, as soon as I'm done instructing these I will go up."

There was a slight pause. "You may return now, Gabriel, thank you," Lucifer said.

"But I'm to escort you."

Lucifer seemed impatient. "Escort me? Why? I mean, very well, that's fine, we'll leave shortly."

An hour later Lucifer finished instructing the angels on musical renditions and orchestrations. As Gabriel and Lucifer ascended the stones of fire to the throne of God, Lucifer looked back upon the Earth. He felt a great sense of accomplishment sweep over him.

My kingdom is a beautiful kingdom and I have made it so. This is my great Eden, that I have built by the might of my power and for the honour of my majesty.

Lucifer took his position behind the Almighty's throne. God stood to create more astrological objects while all of creation praised him. The brightness of the LORD glittered and reflected off the anointed cherub and back upon the sons of God who were watching and praising the LORD. Once the new wonders of the cosmos were created, God sat back down upon his throne and Lucifer left.

"What is it like, Lucifer?" one of the angels asked. "What is it like to stand behind God and reflect his glory?"

"It's wonderful, and I'm humbled to be able to have such a position," Lucifer replied as he and the angel walked through the garden.

"Anyone of us would give anything for an opportunity to do what you do on a regular basis, Lucifer," the angel said. "But we all know that God made you special for the task of showing his glory."

"Yes, he did," Lucifer said while reaching for a piece of fruit.

"Do you have any idea what you look like up there?"

Lucifer took a bite of the fruit and looked squarely and intently at the angel. "I suppose . . ."

Lucifer's voice trailed off for a moment. "I suppose I look like God?"

It was at that moment that something stirred within the mind and heart of Lucifer. A new feeling and emotion came over him. He went from being humble, honored and appreciative of the purpose God had given him to something else entirely.

He felt pride, and it was followed quickly by rebellion.

Lucifer's complexion darkened a little. "Have you ever wondered why God doesn't let you stand behind him?"

The angel was startled at the thought. "I, well, no, I've never even—"

"Have you ever wondered why he created me so unique and failed to do that for you? Have you ever, perhaps, wanted to ask him, 'Why hast thou made me thus'?"

The angel flustered in embarrassment and took a step back.

Lucifer was relentless. "You can be honest with me, friend."

"I suppose I have wondered that," the angel replied. "I mean, I think things would be better if we were all the same. And why did God make Gabriel and Michael different too? Why are there millions of us that are just—"

"I've felt this way for years," Lucifer interrupted. "If I had been the creator I would have done it differently."

The deceiver leaned in, pausing to let his words sink in deeper. "To be honest, and I hesitate a little to say this, but I think I would have done it better."

A feeling of discontentment swelled within the angel as he looked at the dirt by his feet.

Lucifer faked a sense of joviality and slapped the angel on the back. "But what can be done? You have to admit, we do have it pretty good, right?"

"I suppose so."

"Look," Lucifer placed his hand upon the shoulder of his victim. "Yes, if I were in charge up there, as I am down here, everyone would be the same. No one would be higher or lower than anyone else. But I'm not in charge, and that's all there is to it. Nothing can be done about it! There is no point in feeling down about it. Let's enjoy what we have even if it isn't quite right!"

Thinking it was his own idea, the angel went out to recruit other angels to his cause. Within the space of a few days a third of the angels in existence all stood before the throne of Lucifer. Listening to their grievances, he sat contemplative for a few moments. Gazing over the mass of beings before him the angel of light arose from his earthly throne and began to speak.

"I know how you feel. I too have wondered why the LORD did things the way He did," Lucifer said. "Perhaps if we join together and make ourselves as one, we can change things!"

The angels cheered.

Lucifer raised a hand to quiet them. "But what if God does not see things our way? What would you have me to do?"

"Then you will be our god!" the mob cheered.

Lucifer put both his hands up to silence them again. "I have heard your pleas, and I promise I will make things better for all of us one way or another. But I need to know . . . are you with me?"

"Yes! Glory to Lucifer! All hail King Lucifer!"

"Very well," Lucifer said. "I will ascend into heaven and I will exalt my throne above the stars of God."

They roared in response. With his fist held high Lucifer spun and lifted off his throne. "I will sit also upon the mount of the congregation, in the sides of the north: I will ascend above the heights of the clouds. . ."

He paused while floating above his throne and looked at the mass of angels all stunned with excitement and silence before him.

". . . I will be like the most high."

God spoke to Michael. "Do you see what is happening on Earth right now, Michael?"

"Yes Lord, I do."

"What do you think about that?"

Michael placed his hand upon his chest. "I serve and exist for your pleasure, LORD God Almighty, and I seek nothing else. What would you have me to do?"

"Form the other angels into groups; and when I call upon you, cast the Deceiver and his host into the deep."

"Yes, LORD," Michael replied and departed.

Soaring through the cosmos, the rebels approached the great deep. Slicing through the waters, they made their way to the door of the third heaven.

It was closed. That was a first.

Perplexed, they stopped, and in a futile attempt Lucifer tried to open the door. With all the strength he could muster the angel was unable to open the gate to heaven.

The voice of many waters boomed, shaking the universe. "Is this the man that made the earth to tremble? Nay, thou shalt be brought down to hell, to the sides of the pit."

Lucifer tried deception. "Please listen to us, LORD. We have brought you a gift!"

"Friend, betrayest thou the God of Heaven with a kiss? I will cast thee as a profane thing out of the mountain of God: and I will destroy thee, o covering cherub, from the midst of the stones of fire."

Lucifer roared as he began to change shape and form to an enormous red dragon with multiple heads. His heads hissed and moved awkwardly at first, but then reared back and spewed red fire at the door. Having chosen Lucifer as their god, the other angels began to lose their shape as well. They shifted into hideous mutated forms to resemble their new father, Beelzebub.

The LORD of Heaven and Earth spoke. "Ye are gods; and all of you are children of the most high.

But ye shall die like men and fall like one of the princes."

At that moment two massive groups of angels appeared on both sides of the rebels and a war broke out. The angels of God attacked, their blades leaving brilliant streaks of light behind them. They clashed with the demonic horde who countered with claws, fangs and fire.

Confused and disorganized, the fallen angels didn't stand a chance. They were defeated and cast head long into the deep. In the final desperate moments of the battle, bearing his fangs, Satan charged at the weaker Michael who led the assault.

Michael held out his hand. "The LORD rebuke thee, Satan."

With those words ringing in his ears, Satan lost all of his strength and fell backwards, down into the deep with the others. The waters of the deep began to pop and boil with the heat of his rage. Suddenly, the face of the deep between God and Satan froze solid. As if a veil had been placed in the third heaven, separating God from the universe, everything went dark. The universe was destroyed as the deep expanded to flood everything.

And so it was that the Earth was without form and void; and darkness was upon the face of the deep. And the Spirit of God moved upon the face of the waters.

And God said, "Let there be light." And there was light.

And on the sixth day, God said, "Let us make man in our image, after our likeness: and let them have dominion over the fish of the sea, and over the fowl of the air, and over the cattle, and over all the earth, and over every creeping thing that creepeth upon the earth. For I have made him a little lower than the angels, and hast crowned him with glory and honour. I have made him to have dominion over the works of our hands; thou hast put all things under his feet."

The Deceiver burned with fury as he realized his kingdom had been taken from him and given to another.

Chapter Two

"And I will put enmity between thee and the woman, and between thy seed and her seed; it shall bruise thy head, and thou shalt bruise his heel."

Genesis 3:15

4004 B.C.: The Garden of Eden

Following the rebellion, the power and authority over planet Earth had been ripped from Lucifer's grasp and given to a new being named Adam. Adam was the first man created; and the Devil saw him as weak and vulnerable, but the greatest bane of his existence to Satan was that he was made in God's image.

Acting swiftly, Satan deceived the man's wife and now the three of them stood before God in judgment. They were all sinners now; all of them were fallen and unjust. Hence a journey and struggle that would last for thousands of years had just begun. The sky grew dark as they heard their fate. The man and the woman wept as they listened, but the serpent was defiant; this was what he desired. The Earth and everything on it was fallen, filled with the corrupting virus of sin, and by proxy the title deed of Earth fell back into his dark and taloned fingers.

Forced by God to leave the garden, they realized that everything they knew about life was now worthless; it was time to start over in a cruel and unforgiving landscape far different from the happy home they had previously enjoyed. Walking with the garden behind him the man felt the pain of the hard ground beneath his feet. His arm was around his sobbing wife.

That night they heard the noises of the predators acting upon their newly acquired instincts, and their prey screamed as a new fear took hold of them.

"What have we done, Eve . . . what have we done?"

To ensure they never returned to the garden God placed Cherubims, along with a sword of fire, to guard the entrance. Adam and Eve were terrified to go back; and they were terrified to leave, but they had no choice.

Years later, the woman had a baby named Cain. The greatest comfort Eve found was the promise that God gave her about the seed. The seed that one day would bruise the head of the serpent. Maybe when that happened everything would go back to how it had been. Maybe then they could go back home.

Maybe this little boy is the one to bring us back, she thought as she cradled the head of her baby. *Haven't we suffered enough? Maybe God will use him to bring us back to the garden?*

Eve had another son as well and they named him Abel. The boys grew up strong and active. They adapted to the harsh climate very quickly, knowing nothing of the garden other than the campfire stories their parents had told them at night.

Nearly a hundred years came and went from that time in the garden until another terrible day came. Abel bowed before the altar he had built. As he prayed the lamb's blood ran down the wood and onto the earth. A loud blast was heard for miles around and as Abel backed away from the pile of logs a concentrated stream of fire rushed from the heavens and consumed the offering.

He took it! He accepted it! My sins are forgiven! I'm clean!

A few miles away Cain heard the noise and saw the fire. His heart filled with jealousy.

He didn't do anything to deserve that. Anyone can get an animal and kill it. I put time and effort into this and God doesn't appreciate it.

The LORD spoke. "What is the matter, Cain?"

Cain put his head in his hands and cried softly as he stared at the ground. "Why did you accept his sacrifice and not mine? Do you see how much work I put into this?"

"I did not accept it because that is not what I asked for," God replied. "Blood, not fruit, blood. You understand this, Cain. How many times have you and your brother watched as your father showed you how?"

"I know, I know. I just wanted to do better. I know I can do better."

"You can never do any better than what I ask."

"What am I to do now?"

"Go take a lamb from your brother."

The very thought filled Cain with anger. *What I did was better than what he did and now I have to go to him to ask for a new sacrifice?*

"I know you're angry Cain, but I expect the same from you as I do everyone else: obedience. If you obey me, you'll be accepted. If you don't, sin lieth at the door."

Cain half-heartedly began to saunter off to Abel's house to ask his brother if he could have a lamb. It began to grow dark and cold and the evening mist rose to water the ground.

Cain met Abel in the field by his altar. "You're still out here? The fire came and went hours ago."

Abel knew his brother was upset. "I know, but there isn't anything I'd rather do than be out here. This is where we talk."

Cain flushed with resentment but tried to hide it. "Where you talk? You mean you don't just offer the sacrifice? You have conversations with God?"

"Of course, brother! Don't you?"

"Maybe if you want to call being lectured a conversation. I'm tired of feeling like I'm not good enough." Cain stood by the fire warming himself.

Abel sat down and stared into the embers. "None of us are good enough. That's why we offer the sacrifice."

Cain gritted his teeth. "Don't you chide me, Abel. I know what to do and I don't need your help!"

"Calm down."

"Don't tell me to calm down; I didn't walk all the way out here to be told what to do!"

"Then why did you walk out here? Do you want a lamb? Is that why you're here? Are you here because God didn't accept your—"

Cain had all he could take. He grabbed a smoldering piece of timber off the fire and swung it at Abel.

"Cain! What are you doing?!" Abel said as he started to trip. He tried to defend himself but there was no way he could. Cain hit him once and then again and again and again. The blood of Abel ran into the ground as Cain stood over him, out of breath, his heart beating out of his chest. One thought went through his mind: *They'll find him; someone will see what I've done.*

The smell of burning flesh filled the night air as Cain tore through the darkness and fog. He had seen thousands of animals die, but never a man. A fear took hold of his soul that gave him an unreal energy. He stumbled through the night with reckless abandon and no concern for his own safety. His foot caught something and he found himself face first in the mud. Grimacing in pain, he picked himself up and began to hobble off until he slipped and fell again into the sludge.

Exhausted, crying and covered with mud, he fell asleep until the morning.

"Where is your brother Abel?"

Cain woke up, blinded by the sun in his eyes. It was mid-morning and God was talking to him.

"Cain, where is Abel?"

Cain was immediately indignant. "Am I my brother's keeper?"

"Cain, what have you done? The voice of thy brother's blood crieth unto me from the ground. That same ground that took his blood shall no longer feed you and your family. From now on you're a fugitive and vagabond."

Cain was silent for a few moments. "LORD! I can't take this. It's too much. My punishment is more than I can bear! All who see me will try to kill me."

"No Cain, they will not. Everyone will know what you have done, but they will also know that if they try to kill you I'll avenge you seven times."

As Cain headed home a transformation came over him, leaving a mark that would forever identify him as a murderer. When he reached his home Adam was waiting for him.

"How could you, son? God told me what you did. He told me not to come here, but I had to see for myself if it was true."

Cain was beyond feelings at this point. "I guess rebellion runs in the family, doesn't it?"

A tearful rage filled Adam. "Look at you! You're proud of the fact you've killed your brother!"

"That's right," Cain mocked. "Sooner or later someone was going to kill someone around here. It might as well be me - the one on whom all your hopes and dreams lie."

Adam's rage turned to frustration, but Cain never gave him a chance to speak.

"What's that? No more talk about me being the chosen one? Oh, how liberating it is! Please, tell me more about the garden," Cain laughed in mockery of his heartbroken father. "I can't wait to go there! Oh, what's that? It's up to me to bring us there?"

Adam quickly tried to regain his composure. "But—"

"But what? How about, 'I don't know how to fix us all and I don't care anymore!' I've spent the last hundred years with that on my back, and now it's over. I'm not the chosen one. I'm not 'the seed,' and the only place I'm going is to the land of Nod with my wife to start over, however I can. And don't try to follow me."

When the conversation ended and Cain had left, Adam and Eve knew they would never see their oldest son ever again.

But Adam knew his wife again; and she bare a son and called his name Seth: "For God," said she, "hath appointed me another seed instead of Abel, whom Cain slew."

Chapter Three

"And Enoch also, the seventh from Adam,
prophesied of these, saying, Behold, the Lord
cometh with ten thousands of his saints,"
Jude 14

2988 B.C.: Location Unknown

A crowd gathered to listen to the man on the hill. He raised his hand to the heavens as he brought the message of God to the people. "Behold, the Lord cometh with ten thousands of his saints, to execute judgment upon all!"

It was Enoch, one of the few preachers that still remained almost a thousand years after the fall. He stood beseeching the people, pleading with them to repent of their sin and to live right. Some mocked, some listened and some promised to hear him again another day.

When the day came to a close, the preacher went home. As was his custom on the way, he spoke with the LORD. "I surely am looking forward to when you actually do come, LORD. I'm only the seventh from Adam and things are not looking too good around here. When are you going to come, LORD?"

"It is not for you to know the times and seasons, friend. You are doing a good job at speaking my word," the LORD replied.

"Thank you, LORD. I hope you'll forgive me if I'm a little impatient to see you. I don't understand everything you've given me to preach; but if we can see the saints, then I suppose that means we'll be able to see you too when you come with them."

"Enoch," the LORD said, "I love you and I've given you a special revelation that is unique to you. People still do not grasp the idea that I'm actually coming down there personally to make things right."

"LORD, are you saying the seed is—"

Before he could finish the words he was gone; the LORD had taken him.

If one could look past the physical realm and see the things that are invisible to the human eye, one would have seen more than just a man with a message on a hill that day. There was a host of spiritual beings there as well. Tall and strong, the LORD's mighty host stood guard around Enoch as he delivered the words of God. Outside of the ring of angels surrounding the hill, wicked and deformed dark ones clawed and grasped to get through to the preacher. When the message ended and Enoch headed home, they vanished.

All but one: the angel of light remained, the deceiver. Understanding he was not permitted to touch Enoch, Satan still followed him everywhere he went. He was his most loyal listener; the preacher never left his sight. He heard everything the LORD had said to Enoch the day God took him and as he listened the devil began to understand.

Within the calculating mind of the wicked one a plan was set in motion to resist and delay the coming of the seed. The one who was wiser than Daniel reasoned that if the entire Earth were corrupt then there would be no one through whom the seed could come. He saw what was transpiring two thousand years before any prophet of God outside of Enoch had understood it. Satan shuddered as he finally came to the conclusion that the seed of the woman was God himself.

And time, as it does, marched on.

Chapter Four

"But as the days of Noe were, so shall also the coming of the Son of man be."
Matthew 24:37

2299 B.C.: Location Unknown

The Almighty watched through the years as humanity transformed itself into a mongrel race of super beings all bent on power, destruction and wickedness. The sons of God had joined with the daughters of men and their giant offspring fought to rule the world. Great cities had been built, only to be destroyed by hordes of bloodthirsty marauders. Every manner of sexual depravity was rampant and all had been corrupted by strange flesh. Satan had done his job so well that God repented himself of making man.

But Noah found grace in the eyes of the LORD.

"No nails, LORD?" Noah said in bewilderment, "You don't want us to use nails when we build it?"

"No, Noah, use pitch."

"Absolutely, whatever you say LORD."

"Noah, do you remember how an animal had to die because of Adam's sin?"

"Yes, LORD."

"Well," the LORD continued, "everything being used to build this ark is going to be as natural as possible. You're going to have to use saws and hammers to some degree of course, but in the end what I want actually holding this ark together is the blood of a tree. In other words, to save your life and the lives of your family, all the materials that go into this ark will have to come from something that died."

Noah pondered the idea and thought aloud, "Trees."

"That's right, Noah. A tree is going to bear the curse and save your life."

Noah responded without thinking. "You mean 'trees,' right, LORD?"

"No Noah, I meant exactly what I said."

Noah passed the instruction onto his sons and for years they worked tirelessly on building the giant boat. Every day they prayed and asked the LORD for protection and strength; in the middle of the day when the crowds gathered to watch, Noah would find a place to preach.

"You wicked and adulterous generation! God is sending judgment to this land and to this world! You'd better repent! You'd better get right! You'd better turn from your wickedness and serve the LORD, the creator of heaven and Earth!"

They would jeer and laugh. The old guard was gone and Noah had no encouragement outside of his family. Over fifty years before Noah was even born, the last real preacher, Enoch, had been translated and taken to be with God. Adam and Seth had died over five hundred years before.

"You need to turn to God, people! The rain is coming and you don't want to be caught in it! Come to the LORD while time remains!"

As they called back, they showed no respect to the man of God. "What rain? It's never rained before, why will it now? Show us a sign that it will rain. Give us a reason to believe you, Noah! Nothing's ever changed around here and nothing ever will!"

The old man would respond, "A wicked and adulterous generation seeks after a sign! God doesn't owe you a sign, and you have no right to demand one! You've lived in filth and wickedness. Aren't you tired of it? Won't anyone come forward and turn to the LORD?"

Anytime a young man or woman ever felt the urge to come forward to meet Noah, the crowd would erupt in applause and laughter. Embarrassed, they would always slink back, hoping to disappear. But Noah was faithful to preach the word every day, and the people were faithful to reject it.

That is until his family and the animals were entered into the ark. The LORD had shut the door on them and they waited seven days for the rain to come. Miraculously, the animals were as calm and still as Noah's family were for those seven days. They all understood that sudden destruction was nigh.

The doom came pounding from the skies. Sudden mudslides worldwide froze animals into fossils in the middle of eating, playing and everyday life. People fled in panic. Whole families were swept away before they were able to respond. Some made it to the hills and died while holding their children above their heads. The destruction was so vast that the topography of the entire planet was reformed.

The warning had been given and ignored for decades: the judgment of God was coming.

Satan seethed as he watched his corrupted race be wiped out. He grit his teeth knowing that his plan had worked perfectly but for the intervention of God. One man found grace, and one man was all that God needed. Unable to corrupt Noah and Shem, Satan had done nothing to stop the coming of the seed.

Chapter Five

"And Cush begat Nimrod: he began to be a mighty
one in the earth."
Genesis 10:8

2144 B.C.: Not Far From Shinar

Joban and his son felt the heat of the day weigh down on them as they worked the ground.

"When are we going to be done, Father?" Ared said.

Joban wiped the sweat from his burning eyes. "Soon, boy, soon."

Ared disliked being called a boy; he fancied himself a man. He never let on that he felt this way, of course, but he did nonetheless. The heat was getting to him, but he was strong and could take it. It was the time of year when he and his father would take a break and work again at night before it grew too dark.

On the way home they talked. "Do you think the stories of the warrior are true?"

"Of course not, son. There is only one true God and he's still alive and well," the father replied.

"Okay, Father. I guess when you hear everyone saying it over and over again sometimes you start believing it yourself. Just the idea alone of a man hunting down the LORD and killing him is crazy. . ." he trailed off.

Joban nodded. "A mighty hunter is one thing, but—"

He was cut short by a club across the back of the head. He went down in a heap as a net was cast across his son. Ared quickly squirmed out of it and ran toward his father, throwing his shoulder against the man that was bending over him. They rolled around in the dirt for a short period of time until the others had subdued him. Two more drug him off the ground and spun him towards a much larger man who immediately hit him across the face.

"No, Father, help," he cried as everything went black.

"Wake up," a voice said as Ared and his father were roughly awakened, each by a kick in the side. "Get up!"

Blinded by the glare of sunlight and nauseated from hunger pains, the two staggered to their feet. Others in the fenced area were gathering to see a man carried on a throne; its weight spread over two beams and being borne by large men. He was escorted by a gaudy procession. Some fanned him with huge leaves; others played music, convulsing in wild syncopated rhythms. Warriors walked before him waving all manner of weapons. Finally, the drums stopped and the company halted.

The man, dressed in the leopard skins, arose and called to the captives. "Welcome to Shinar and welcome to the glorious future that awaits you!"

A prisoner in front started to respond but was interrupted by the glistening tip of a spear on his chest. "Know your place. Don't interrupt his majesty," the large bearded warrior hissed, his eyes communicating to the prisoner his need to listen.

"My name is Nimrod, and I have been given power by the sun-god. With great vengeance for all who've suffered, I have slain the God of the flood and together we will take his throne!"

Those around him cheered and chanted mantras of victory. Nimrod raised his hand and they stopped.

"I now lay before you a choice: life or death. You can start your life over in my kingdom, or you can die now. Choose life, work hard and when our tower is built you will share in the glory of it!"

Wide-eyed, Ared glanced over to his father who quickly put his finger to his lips, motioning that he should remain quiet. Across from them, another young man was attempting to slip through the slats. He made it through and the dirt kicked up behind his feet as he ran for his life.

"I am Nimrod," he said as an arrow snapped free from his bow, "the mighty hunter."

Several days later the angel of the LORD stood upon the ground watching the group of prisoners join the thousands already working on the tower. There were people from all over the Earth; some had come from the East for a new life, others were forced to be there against their will, yet they all worked together to construct an edifice in blasphemy against the true God.

"Here to ruin all the fun again?" A dark being said as he materialized next to the LORD.

"I see you are doing what you do best: imitating me," the Almighty replied.

Satan smiled. "That's right; I know you can't bear to let this go without getting in the middle of it at some point. But I've laid the foundation already to subvert what you're planning. This will be my kingdom—"

The LORD cut him off. "The kingdom in which people will love and worship you for all eternity?"

"I don't care about any of that! I already know where you're going in this game, and I'm going to beat you to the spot. Before you're ever born into this world, I will already have filled the Earth with legends and stories of mother-child gods. Your birth won't be noticed and no one will ever worship your human form. They won't accept you because your story will have already been told a thousand times over by savages and idolaters years before you arrive."

The LORD continued to watch the construction, unsurprised by Lucifer's words. "Take advantage of the head start I am giving you. A thousand years is as a day to me and you don't have many days left until my day comes."

Satan tried to speak, but his voice caught in his throat when the Almighty raised his hand. Behind the devil there was a commotion as tempers began to flare within the city. The LORD had confounded the languages and Nimrod's kingdom was never the same. Satan turned to see riots and fights break out. By the end of the day people had begun to form into groups and abandon the work.

Ared sat weeping as he watched the sun set on the horizon. His father was gone. He had searched all day within the camp of Babel and found nothing. He made the assumption that Joban had been taken off by slave traders.

But God had other plans. Behind the weeping boy came Joban, dirty and bruised, guided by a guardian angel. He placed his hand on his son's shoulder and they embraced.

"Where have you been?" Ared asked.

"Someplace terrible. Nimrod's religion . . . this sun-god worship," he struggled to talk. "I'm just glad the LORD delivered me when he did."

"Me too, Father, me too. I'll never doubt him again."

Satan's initial rule had been brought down at Babel, but the great imitator was undaunted. He knew he had laid the groundwork for his future counterfeit kingdom. Nimrod's widow, Semiramis, married her son and began a blasphemous and incestuous mother-child deity religion that would take on many forms throughout time.

Chapter Six

"And spared not the old world, but saved Noah the eighth *person*, a preacher of righteousness, bringing in the flood upon the world of the ungodly;"

II Peter 2:5

1977 B.C.: Ur of the Chaldees

"Is that the absurd temple you were telling me about, Shem?" Noah said as his aging eyes squinted to look at the enormous structure.

"Yes, Father, there it is: the temple of the moon god and his wife."

Noah gingerly stepped off the boat and onto the dock. "I'm so tired of this Nimrod garbage. Sometimes I wish God would just flood everything all over again."

"Actually," Shem said, "Nimrod's religion, the worship of the sun-god, is across the river at Babylon. Here they worship several false gods but in particular they follow after the moon-god, Nanna, who was the illegitimate child of Ninlil the air goddess."

Noah just looked at him and blinked. "Goodnight, could you be any more . . . oh, never mind."

Noah had no use for Shem's exposition on various religions; he was grumpy and tired. "Maybe God could just torch them all."

Shem smiled. "It is certainly a good thing that God is much kinder than you father, or nothing would remain of the Earth – every fifty years!"

"I know, I know," Noah said as he observed the line of people paying taxes at the temple. "I'm just tired of preaching to people and never seeing anything happen. I know the results are up to God, but sometimes this feels like a job and not a calling."

Then the old grizzled preacher sighed. "When is the seed coming?"

Shem's eyes locked onto his father's with a look of understanding. "Your resiliency has always been an inspiration to me, father."

"Well," Noah said, "this place is as good a place as any. Here we go."

Noah faced the crowd; and with a voice like thunder not normally found in a man his age, he began to preach.

"My name is Noah, and I am a preacher of righteousness. I serve the LORD God, who flooded this world and confounded the languages at Babylon. It's only by His mercy He doesn't torch this place and destroy all of you for your idolatry! You worship pieces of wood and rock that can't see, talk, or move – but I serve the God that created the wood and rock. Repent!"

Noah took a break and then Shem preached for a while. The people mocked and ignored the men; a few remained afterwards to argue. The crowd dispersed eventually, and the two men sat down under a tree, exhausted.

"Would you like something to drink, sir?" a boy said as he handed a cup of water to Noah. "You look a little tired."

The old saint of God looked at the little boy in front of him and thought he saw something special. The little boy knew that he saw something different in Noah.

Noah smiled and took the cup. "Well, young man, I'm not as spry as I used to be. Thank-you."

"You're welcome, sir."

Shem jumped in. "What do you think about all of this, boy?"

"Well, I don't know. My father has an idol shop on the other side of town; I've spent my whole life around them. My family worships them."

Compassionately Noah spoke up with his gravelly voice. "Have they ever done anything for you, son? Have any of those statues ever done anything for you?"

"No, sir."

"My God forgave me of my sins. Did any of those gods forgive you of your sins?"

"No, sir."

"Son, if you want to start worshiping the real God, you can call out to him anytime you want, anywhere you want. He loves you more than you'll ever know, and he wants to forgive you of your sins. He even wants to be your friend."

"That sounds good, I'll think about it. I have to go now; my father wants me to watch the shop while he runs some errands."

As the boy turned to run off, Noah called after him, "What's your name, boy?"

"Abram, and my father's name is Terah."

The entire time the boy ran home, he thought about what the old man and his son had said. The gods in his father's store did nothing but sit there until some fool came to buy one. The best they could do for him was to make the family a little bit of money, but even then it was the skilled craftsmanship of his father that made them the money. The LORD had already prepared Abram for this truth, but the war for his soul was raging within him all the way home.

"Take care of the shop while I'm gone, son," Terah said as he walked out the door. "I'll be back soon."

When the boy was alone, he picked up a rod and walked over to one of the little statutes on a shelf. With his nose about three inches away from it, he just stared.

"Are you for real?"

Abram waited for a response.

"Do something."

Nothing happened.

"Ok, you had your chance," Abram said as he knocked the image off the shelf and watched it shatter on the ground.

Abram looked at the next statue. "You had better say something, mister, or that's what's going to happen to you."

A quick swing of the staff took the idol's head right off. One by one Abram destroyed every statue in the room, giving them all a chance to speak up for themselves first.

A half hour later Terah returned. "What in the world have you done here, son?"

"I didn't do anything. You might not believe this but he did it," Abram said, pointing to the fat idol in the corner. "The big one took that stick and broke all the other idols. I guess he was jealous or something."

"I don't believe that, Abram! Why did you do this!"

Abram looked at his father. "Why do you think I did it?"

"Because an idol can't go walking around knocking over other statutes and beating them with sticks. Idols can't do anything."

Abram looked at his father squarely in the face. "Then why do we worship them, Father? Why do we worship them?"

"What else are we supposed to do, son?"

"A man told me today about the God of the flood: a God who can really forgive sins. There was something different about him. When he spoke in the marketplace, he told everyone that he's actually spoken with this God and that he's the one true God. Why don't we worship him, Father?"

Terah's irritation with his son turned to heartfelt consideration for a few moments as he stared at the ground. Terah knew what the boy was saying was true, and the Holy Spirit bore witness to his heart of the true God.

"Well, we might as well," Terah said as he gave the last remaining idol a shove. "I don't want to have to remake these all over again, anyways."

That day revival came to the house of Terah, the father of Abram. And because of his decision to serve the one true God, the world was forever changed.

Chapter Seven

"For all the land which thou seest, to thee will I give
it, and to thy seed for ever."
Genesis 13:15

1891 B.C.: Between Haran and Bethel

"**D**on't you think we're a little old for this, Abram?" Sarai said with a smile.

Abram tried to maintain an upbeat attitude. "What are you talking about, lady? I feel as strong as I did when I was thirty and you look just as good!"

"I don't feel like I'm thirty; I'll tell you that," Sarai responded.

Surrounded by dirt and sand as far as the eye could see, Abram thought back over the last few decades. He remembered God's command and promise unto him.

Get thee out of thy country, and from thy kindred, and from thy father's house, unto a land that I will show thee: and I will make of thee a great nation, and I will bless thee, and make they name great; and thou shalt be a blessing. I will bless them that bless thee, and curse him that curseth thee: and in thee shall all families of the earth be blessed.

That was a long time ago. Abram sighed when he thought of the wasted years and energy spent in Haran. After his older brother had died in Ur, Abram decided to leave. Already saddened that he had lost one son, Terah decided to come as well. And Lot, who was the son of Abram's dead brother, came along also.

Abram remembered how God had commanded him to leave his family behind. He understood all too well how much time he had wasted for not obeying that command. Seeing the eager Lot in front of him caused him to wince at the idea of what might lay ahead because of his partial obedience. He put the thoughts in the back of his mind and tried to ignore them. God had made a personal and amazing promise to him and on that he was going to focus.

"We should be arriving at Luz soon," Abram said.

"Good," Sarai said with a hint of snideness in her voice. "I could use a break. Dear brother."

Sarai was still a little bent over Abram's gaffe back in Egypt.

Abram felt a little dejected. "How many times do I have to say I'm sorry about that? I can't do anything about it now."

"You can stop apologizing, Abram," Sarai said with a smile. "I'm just so happy I have such a brave brother to take care of me."

At this point Abram decided that discretion was in fact the better part of valour. Abram had always been the type to avoid confrontation; that tendency and also a lapse in faith is what put him into trouble in Egypt. Sarai wasn't keen on the idea of pretending that Abram was her brother, but went along with it. Abram justified it because she was in fact his half-sister, but Pharaoh and rest of the eligible bachelors in Egypt didn't quite see it that way.

Satan used Abram's faithlessness to try to pollute Abram's line, but God intervened by plaguing Pharaoh's house. Sarai was returned to Abram by Pharaoh; and they left with Lot, as well as a generous love offering courtesy of the rulers of Egypt.

"I guess you could say all things work together for good, Sarai," Abram said, ending the conversation.

Over the process of time, Abram and his family reached Luz and began to dwell in the land of Canaan. The LORD had dealt with Abram concerning his lack of faith in Egypt, and Abram purposed in his heart not to let it happen again.

"We have to do something about this," Lot said as he stood by Abram watching a couple of their servants argue from a distance.

"I know. It's starting to get out of hand. It seems like we're dealing with this sort of thing every day now."

"What should we do?"

Abram was silent for a moment. "Lot, we have to go our separate ways."

Lot was startled. "What do you mean? I thought we were going to stick this out to the end!"

"I'm sorry Lot. I wasn't supposed to bring you in the first place. God told me to leave my kindred, but I brought you and Father along with me. I'm sure God has a plan for you too, if you're willing to obey him and follow him."

Lot shuffled his feet and looked up at Abram.

"We can't stay together, Lot," Abram continued. "If we do, our herdsmen are going to keep fighting. Sooner or later you and I will start fighting. Look around. You take whatever land you want, and I'll take the rest. If you take the right, I'll take the left; take the left, and I'll take the right. You have the first choice."

Lot lifted up his eyes and beheld the plain of Jordan, that it was well watered. "I guess I'll go there."

Abram's heart sunk within him as he watched Lot walk away.

Lord, is this what you have for me? First my father and now my nephew is gone. I don't understand. How is this is a blessing?

The LORD interrupted his thoughts. "Abram, Lot made his decision based on what he saw. Now I'd like for you to look around."

Abram looked up at hearing the voice of God.

"Abram," the LORD continued, "everything you see is yours. I'm giving it to you and your seed forever. Look to the north, the south, east, west – it's all yours, friend. In fact, I'm going to make your seed as the dust of the Earth, everything you see here will one day be yours."

Chapter Eight

"Without father, without mother, without descent, having neither beginning of days, nor end of life; but made like unto the Son of God; abideth a priest continually."

Hebrew 7:3

1884 B.C.: Hebron

"Giants?" the chief servant said. "I thought they all perished in the flood!"

Abram slapped a sheathed sword into the man's hand. "Apparently not or somehow they came back, but either way they've captured Lot."

One servant in the back whispered to another, "They can keep him. What chance do we have against giants?"

Abram turned to face him. "We'll do just fine; we have the LORD on our side."

Abram's men stood staring at him, hoping for a plan.

"A smaller force can defeat a larger army if it utilizes stealth and trickery. We're not going to face them in broad daylight. This is a night raid."

"So we're going to go in, recover Lot, and escape out of there, right?"

"No, the family of Abram is going to war against the trained armies of four different nations tonight. We're going to destroy their armies and save Lot and his family."

"Are you sure about this, sir? There's about three hundred of us—"

"Three hundred and eighteen, plus the LORD," Abram interrupted.

"Right," the chief servant recovered, "and there's about twenty thousand of them."

Abram looked the servant in the eye. "Is it anything to the LORD to save by many, or by a few? Is anything too hard for God? Would he have us to sit here idly as my nephew and his family are sold into slavery, or worse? God has called us to be men of action. He said he would bless them that bless me and that he would curse them that curse me."

The servant slunk back and Abram turned to face the other servants and raised his sword high into the air. "Gentlemen, tonight we will test the strength of the promises of God! He will not fail us, and we will not fail him!"

The sentries outside the camp didn't see what hit them, and what hit each one of them was an arrow in the neck. A bizarre dampening of their senses had taken place that fateful evening. A thick fog hung in the air as thousands of soldiers slept a sleep from which they would never awake. Abram's men stole into the camp from every direction, slipping in and out of the tents, leaving nothing but bloody corpses behind them.

Eventually, what was bound to happen happened. Someone tripped, knocked over a spear or broke something by accident. A noise was made and the enemy was awakened. The soldiers of Abram froze in place, expecting what would naturally follow.

But what followed was supernatural.

The enemy camp was in disarray. Nothing seemed to go right as men screamed in frustration at each other. All chain of command had been lost. Where there were ten soldiers together, Abram had thirty there to slay them. When hundreds of enemy soldiers would manage to band together to form an offensive they would charge screaming headlong into the darkness, only to slay another regiment of their own fellow soldiers who were blinded by their own confusion.

The only semblance of order was to stampede from the camp like a herd of cattle. Those who survived the slaughter in the camp ran madly into the night. Thousands fled in the mass confusion, with nothing to light their way but their own wild imaginations of what was happening. Reaching the valley of Shaveh, hundreds tripped and fell over each other, skewering themselves on their own weapons. Those who managed to maintain their balance and footing flocked into the bottom of the valley, only to look up and see what appeared to be thousands of lights on the rim above them. There was about a hundred and fifty soldiers waiting for them, but the cursed enemy saw many more than that.

"The sword of the LORD and of Abram!" the soldiers on the hilltop roared as the arrows rained down on the enemy. The enemy turned to flee in fear, many of them inadvertently stabbing each other or falling on their own sharpened weapons. There was no escaping the valley as arrows rained death upon them all.

"I can't believe this, Abram. Thank you for saving us," the king of Sodom said.

"Thank the LORD," Abram replied as he stood looking at the sunrise.

"Well, of course," the king said. "Can you thank him for me?"

"You wouldn't have been in this mess to begin with, King, if you knew the LORD yourself."

The king was polite, but a little annoyed. "Abram, my religion is my business. You have your religion and I have mine."

"And how good was yours when you needed it? Three hundred of the LORD's men just defeated an army seven times its size. That's what my God can do for me."

"Abram, I am very grateful for everything you've done for me and my people. Feel free to keep all the spoil; whatever you find is yours. Just let us go in peace."

Abram flushed with righteous indignation at the king of Sodom for his flippant attitude to the LORD. "I don't even want a shoelace from you. My men ate some of the food they found, but other than that you may take all your things and go. I don't want you to return saying that Abram became rich off of you.

What I did I did for the LORD and to save my nephew Lot. Your people happened to be in the right place at the right time. Last night you saw both the mercy of God and the judgment of God. I suggest you do something about the wickedness of your nation, or one day you'll wind up on the wrong side of the one who holds your very breath in his hands."

As the king of Sodom stormed away, a hooded figure passed by him and stood before Abram.

The stranger held out bread and wine for Abram to take. "Blessed be Abram of the most high God, possessor of heaven and earth: and blessed be the most high God, which hath delivered thine enemies into thy hand."

"Amen. It's always good to meet a fellow believer," Abram replied.

They both sat down and the stranger pulled back his hood. "I am Melchizedek, a prophet, priest and king of the most high God."

"You look familiar," Abram said and took a bite of the bread.

"We may have met before," the king of Salem said with a smile as he reached for a piece.

The two sat together that morning, watching the sunrise and sharing a meal. This king of Salem,

Melchizedek, was a greater man than Abram, and Abram gave him a tithe of everything he owned.

Just as the stranger was a figure clouded in mystery throughout the ages, so too was the conversation these great men had that day. They spoke of things that only the priest of the most high God and the friend of God would understand. They spoke of the promised seed of the woman and the LORD's promises to Abram.

"Eve never saw her promised realized. Will I ever see mine?" Abram asked.

"There are things I can tell you and things I cannot, Abram," the king replied. "God's promises are faithful and true. Eve will receive her promise, and so will you. In fact, you can't have one without the other.

"You have a long and weary road ahead of you, my friend, but stay true and obey the LORD. The day will come when people will look to you as a great example of faith. There's a spiritual kingdom coming and a physical one. You're going to be the father of both of them."

And with that, the man stood and walked off into the morning mist, never to be seen again by Abram.

Chapter Nine

"And he said unto him, I *am* the LORD that brought thee out of Ur of the Chaldees, to give thee this land to inherit it."
Genesis 15:7

The Evening of the Next Day: Hebron

The family of Abram and Lot rejoiced together, celebrating the great victory the LORD had brought them. There was music and a great feast as the servants were laughing and telling stories by campfires. Where there had once been strife between the hired help of these two men, there was now unity, fellowship and joy.

Abram took Lot aside. "Brother, you need to leave that place."

Lot, still smiling, was a little confused. "What do mean, what are you talking about?"

"You need to leave Sodom. God has told me over and over again that the place is wicked. It's only a matter of time before he judges it."

"What? What do you mean?"

"What I mean is that God is going to do something terrible to that place! You're not safe there."

"Oh," Lot said, "look, everything is fine, okay? Sodom isn't any different than any other town."

"You know that's not true," Abram said with concern in his eyes. "I'm telling you, you need to leave there before it's too late. I don't know if I'll be able to save you next time."

Lot looked upon his uncle with appreciation for everything he had done for him. "Thank you, Abram; I'll give it some prayer."

"You don't need to pray. When God's will is clear you need to act."

"I understand; and I thank you, Abram, but I'm just not ready yet."

Abram looked into Lot's eyes for a moment and then turned to walk outside. When he was by himself, Abram began to pray for his family and for his nephew's family.

"Fear not, Abram," the LORD said. "I am thy shield and thy exceeding great reward."

"LORD," Abram replied, "what will you give me? I have no children. Even if you give me all the land you promised me, what good is it without any children with whom to leave it?"

"Abram," the LORD spoke tenderly, "remember last time you operated by faith and not sight, and you let Lot pick first?"

"Yes, LORD."

"Well, I had you look around, and I made you a promise based on what you saw."

"Yes, LORD."

"I want you to look again now, only I want you to look up. What do you see, Abram?"

"I see stars, LORD. The sky is filled with them."

"Tell the stars; can you count them?"

"No, LORD."

"Abram, those are your children. If you can count them, that's your seed. I am going to make your children as the stars of heaven. What do you think about that?"

"I believe you, LORD."

"But you're an old man, Abram, much too old to have children. Do you still believe me?"

"Yes, LORD. If you said it, I believe it."

"Do you know, Abram, that people are going to think you're crazy for believing me? Who in his right mind is going to believe that a man your age can have children?"

"No one would believe that rag-tag army of mine could do what it did either, LORD," Abram said with a smile as he gazed up into the night sky.

"How's it feel to have faith in my promises, friend?"

"It feels wonderful, LORD," Abram said, his eyes welling up.

"Not only am I going to make your seed as the stars of heaven, but for believing me I'm going to give you my righteousness. It's yours now and all you had to do to receive it was believe me."

"Thank you LORD, thank you."

The next day the LORD communed again with Abram. He showed him another sign to demonstrate that he would give him the land as an inheritance. All day long the LORD spoke with Abram concerning these matters; and in the evening, Abram slept as a horror of great darkness descended upon him.

"Abram, you will have a seed, but the day will come that they will be a stranger in a land that is not theirs. They're going to be slaves for four hundred years, but then they will come out again with great substance and riches

after I judge that nation. You will die in peace, but four generations of your seed are going to struggle in bondage until I send them a prophet to deliver them. While this is going on, I'm going to be giving the inhabitants of the land, Canaan land, more space to repent. The iniquity of the Amorites is not yet full."

The next day the LORD continued to reveal himself to Abram. Making a covenant with Abram, God unconditionally promised to give all of the land from the river of Egypt to the river Euphrates to his seed. God had promised to give to Abram's seed over three hundred thousand square miles of land.

Plenty of room for a kingdom.

Chapter Ten

"And Sarai Abram's wife took Hagar her maid the
Egyptian, after Abram had dwelt ten years in the
land of Canaan, and gave her to her husband Abram
to be his wife."
Genesis 16:3

1864 B.C.: Hebron

Fifteen years had come and gone since that fateful day that Abram, the father of faith, took matters into his own hands. The friend of God who had enjoyed daily communion with the LORD, went thirteen years without hearing his voice because of a lapse in faith.

Desperate for a son, Sarai had convinced Abram to wed her handmaiden Hagar. A baby was born to the family and they called his name Ishmael. Abram was eighty-six years old when the baby was born and God didn't speak to him again until he was ninety-nine.

Abraham thought back on the day that God broke the silence to him: *I am the Almighty God; walk before me and be thou perfect.*

That was the same day that God changed his name to Abraham and Sarai's name to Sarah. He was shocked when God told him that Ishmael was not going to be the promised seed and that the seed would come from a baby born of Sarah. That baby's name was Isaac and he was about a year old now; Abraham was one hundred.

Abraham's thoughts were drawn into his present dilemma. *I put myself into this mess to begin with by obeying my wife and now I'm supposed to turn around and start listening to her again?*

"That's right," the LORD said, reading his thoughts. "The boy has to go."

"But LORD, he's my son! I love him!"

"I know you do Abraham. I'm going to take care of him; but he is not the heir, and he and his mother must leave."

"But last time she left you wanted her to come back!"

"Abraham, you need to trust me. I'm going to take care of Ishmael. He is going to be the father of a great nation, because he is of your seed."

"I'll miss him, LORD. I'll miss him."

Abraham didn't sleep at all that night. He lay there staring up into the night sky, thinking about his oldest son. He remembered the day he was born, his first steps. He remembered watching as one of his servants taught Ishmael to shoot a bow and then listening to the boy tell him how one day he was going to drag his father out on a hunting trip when he was older. These thoughts plagued and haunted Abraham all night.

Then the morning came.

"We're going to die, Abraham," Hagar said as she looked him in the face. "Is this what you want?"

"Of course not."

"Why are you so willing to do what she says?"

"I'm not. I'm doing what God says."

The boy interrupted. "Father, are we going to die? Why do we have to go? I don't understand. What's going on?"

Abraham's heart broke again. "My boy, I don't know how to say this, but God has a special plan for you and a special plan for your baby brother. God is going to take care of you and your mother but you have to leave."

"But where are we going to go to and why aren't you coming with us?"

"I don't know where you're going; God is going to lead you and you must trust him. I don't know if I'll ever see you again. I'm very old, son, and I don't have much time left."

"But I don't like this! I don't want to go."

Abraham stared at his son for a few moments. "I'm so sorry, son," he said. "But these are the consequences of sin. Do you remember the first time you saw Eliazar bring back a dead animal?"

"Yes."

"That animal died because of sin. Everyone dies because of sin. We all suffer because of sin and sometime we wind up in terrible spots because of sin. Many times it is the ones who did nothing wrong that have to suffer because of sin, son. You and your mother have to leave here because of my sin. I'm sorry. This is my fault."

The fifteen-year old boy was shocked as he and his mother turned and walked away.

The sand burned their eyes as it swept up off the ground. It had been three days since they had left and the exposure from the sun was killing them. The water had run out that morning and at this point they were merely stumbling along. Hagar was leaning on her boy for strength and at times he was leaning on her. They were exhausted, dehydrated and starving. By divine protection, they had managed to avoid robbers, slave traders and wild animals; but they had also failed to discover any source of food or water.

"We're going to die," she breathed through cracked lips.

Ishmael's strength gave out and he collapsed into the sand, bringing his mother down with him. She lay there for a few moments, but her protective maternal instincts kicked in and she began to fight to get on her feet. Using every ounce of strength in her frail body, she drug the boy over to a shrub to shade him from the sun.

He's not going to wake up, but at least he'll be in the shade.

Hagar knew this was the end and she didn't want to leave this world with the last image in her mind being the death of her son. Abandoning all hope, she crawled as far as she could away from the boy. She propped herself up with her back to a giant boulder, weeping for what seemed like hours.

Awakened out of her sleep, Hagar looked around confused. She was disoriented. Fighting her way through the mental fog she discerned the faltering voice of her son.

"Mother, I'm thirsty . . . Mother, where are you? Did you leave me? Mother . . ."

Everything within her screamed to respond to her boy's call. He was a strong young man, but he was still her baby boy and she would give her life for him. She hopelessly realized that she had no strength to move.

Then the LORD spoke. "What aileth thee Hagar? Fear not, I have heard the voice of thy son. Go to your son and hold him, for I will make of him a great nation."

Finding a sudden surge of strength within her, Hagar lifted up her eyes and saw a well of water. Pulling herself up to her feet she staggered over to the water. She gently touched it to her lips and began to drink. She scrambled over to her son and gave him drink as well.

"He was right," the boy said. "God did take care of us."

Chapter Eleven

"I find then a law, that, when I would do good, evil
is present with me."
Romans 7:21

1834 B.C.: The Land of Moriah

F ifteen more years had come and gone since the day that Ishmael and his mother left. Abraham was now a giant of faith, having seen God deliver him and take care of his family over and over again. The friend of God had many personal conversations with the LORD over the years and the LORD had told him how Ishmael had grown up to be an archer and a great leader.

And now after all these years had passed since God had asked for one boy to go, he was asking Abraham to kill his other son: the promised seed of the kingdom.

Take now thy son, thine only son Isaac, whom thou lovest, and get thee into the land of Moriah; and offer him there for a burnt offering upon one of the mountains which I will tell thee of.

That night Abraham kept replaying it in his mind, over and over again. They had been on the trip now for two days since that terrible message was given. For two days he hadn't heard from God; his last orders were to sacrifice his son. *How could He ask me to do something like this? God, are you there? Why, LORD?*

Abraham tossed and turned in agony. The fifth cherub leaned over him and jammed a spiritual dart straight into his heart. *What kind of God do you serve, old man? Why are you even out here? What kind of loving God gives you two children and then takes them both away from you? Where are you supposed to get all those descendents from if you kill their father?*

Abraham sobbed as he lay there enveloped by the spiritual darkness. He had once gone thirteen years without hearing from God because of a lack of faith and now he wasn't hearing from God during his greatest test of faith.

"Is everything okay, Father?" Isaac interrupted; he was lying on the ground on the other side of the fire. "I thought I heard something."

"What? Oh, son, come here," Abraham said as he hugged his boy and wept.

"Why are you crying, Father?"

Abraham gathered himself. "Isaac, my boy, I'm an old man and sometimes old men cry. Now go back to bed. We have a long trip that we must make tomorrow."

"Are you sure you're okay?"

"Yes, son. I'm fine. Now rest."

As Isaac returned to sleep, Abraham turned away and hid his face in the darkness. The fire warmed his back as the pain and confusion tore him apart on the inside. *At least I know Ishmael is alive, but Isaac, my heir, my precious boy—*

Another dart struck deep. *—God wants him dead. This isn't faith, Abraham, it's foolishness! Why would God tell you to do this? God doesn't tell you to do this, Satan does! If God isn't willing that any should perish, why would He tell you to kill your own boy, the boy upon which all his promises hinge? Quit this foolishness!*

All night long the battle raged within the heart of the old man. Anger, bitterness, frustration, helplessness, and doubt – they all hit him at various times. Satan was his constant companion and tears were his only defense.

Tears and faith, for the old soldier would bend, but he would not break.

"Will he make it, LORD?" Michael said as the host of Heaven watched the battle from above.

"He'll make it, Michael. That's my friend Abraham; he won't let me down."

"Why don't you help him, LORD?"

"Michael," the LORD spoke, "at this point it's simply about believing what I have said. He knows the truth; he knows what I've promised him, and he knows me."

Michael nodded. "Never doubt in the darkness what you've been shown in the light."

"That's right. I fight for my people, and I intervene on their behalf when they are young; but when they are old, many times they must fight on their own. It's at that point they go from trusting in my miracles to trusting in my promises."

"I see."

"What Abraham understands and what countless other saints will understand when they hear of Abraham is that my grace has kept them safe thus far. My grace will lead them home."

Isaac was confused. Something was wrong with his father since the day they left, but he couldn't quite place it. He caught his father crying to himself several times. Many times he would say something to his father and would have to repeat it a couple times before he would respond. His father was deep in thought, struggling with something, but he wasn't talking about it.

As they headed up the mount, Isaac tried to get his father's attention. Abraham's thousand-yard stare was stronger than ever now.

"Father?"

"I'm sorry. Yes son?"

"We have the fire and wood, but where is the lamb?"

Abraham stopped walking for a moment and faced his son. His eyes looked right through the boy.

"My son, God will provide himself a lamb for a burnt offering," Abraham said and then turned to proceed up the mount.

"Don't you mean that God will provide for us a lamb?"

Abraham kept right on walking, unaware of his son's reply or of his own prophetic statement.

At the top of the mountain, Abraham and his son began to build the altar.

"This one is going to be bigger than normal, son," Abraham said. "We need to make it long enough for about three lambs."

Isaac's confusion had reached its tipping point.

"What's going on? You've been acting strange this whole trip. Can you please tell me what is going on?"

Abraham could contain himself no longer and wept aloud. He fell to his knees in front of the boy and covered his face with his hands. The sound of the man's sobbing was carried by the afternoon air up to the third heaven where the fifth cherub stood before the throne of God.

"He's going to quit!" Satan said.

"Just like Enoch and Noah?" the LORD replied.

Isaac helped his father stand back up. "It's okay, Father."

"No it's not, son. It's not!"

Satan laughed as the host of heaven watched the battle continue.

"Son, God told me to kill you!" Abraham cried. "He told me to sacrifice you on this altar. I have to do this, my boy! I don't know why he told me to, but I know he did! God's promises are real, and he must be willing to raise you from the dead if needed – but you have to die first!"

To say Isaac was stunned would be an understatement.

Satan smiled and turned to face the throne. "If you'll excuse me, I think I'll go visit that young man for a moment."

Isaac stood staring off into the valley as his father tried to gather himself. On instinct alone, almost mindlessly, he began to pick up more stones for the altar.

Then the darts found a new victim. *He's really lost it now! God didn't tell him that! The heathen do human sacrifices, not believers!*

The young man's eyes turned from being glossed over to focusing on his father, as another dart struck him hard. *Look at him, he's an old man. You don't have to go along with this. It's not as though he can make you do it! No one is going to blame you if you stop this madness. Your father will thank you later.*

Isaac began to give in. "Father, I..."

That's it! Tell him he's crazy! Tell him you're going to start looking for a real lamb to kill, and that he needs to take a seat. Tell him!

"Father, I think you need to sit down."

"What, son?"

"It's been a long trip, Father. Please sit down and rest. I'll build the altar and then you can do what the LORD told you to do."

Satan cursed for rage as he watched the son of Abraham build the very altar upon which he was to be slain. He was stunned to see the boy then lay across the altar, as his father bound his hands and his feet.

"Son, thank you for not fighting me on this. I know this is what God wants."

"God hasn't let us down yet. I don't think he's going to now."

"If we don't have his promises," Abraham said as looked into the boy's eyes, "then we don't have anything."

"I know Father, but if there be any way—" he paused. "Nevertheless, not what I will, but what thou wilt."

With that, the old man raised the knife high in the air. He wanted it to be finished with one strike. He had no intention of bludgeoning his son to death upon the altar.

The sharpened blade flashed in the sunlight and came down strong and fast.

Abraham's wrist struck something hard and invisible and it knocked the knife to the dirt.

"Abraham, Abraham," the LORD said from Heaven.

"Yes, LORD?"

"Lay not thy hand upon the lad, neither do thou any thing unto him: for now I know that thou fearest God, seeing thou hast not withheld thy son, thine only son from me."

It was almost more than the old man could handle. Materializing before him, an angel of God stood by the altar and he held Abraham's wrist in his hand.

The angel smiled. "Your son is going to be just fine."

Abraham staggered backwards in a daze. His eyes glossed over and in a brief moment of time images flashed before him. He saw the kingdom. He saw himself, Isaac and Isaac's son there. He saw the king in his glory. He saw the kings of the Gentile nations come and worship. He saw people partake of the tree that Adam and Eve were forbidden.

The vision faded as quickly as it had come; and Abraham caught sight of a ram caught by its horns in a thicket, almost as though it wore a crown of thorns.

The angel cut Isaac free and disappeared as Abraham worked to bring the ram over to the altar.

The LORD continued speaking. "In blessing I will bless thee, and in multiplying I will multiply thy seed as the stars of the heaven, and as the sand which is upon the sea shore; and thy seed shall possess the gate of his enemies; And in thy seed shall all the nations of the earth be blessed; because thou hast obeyed my voice."

That day the boy and his father praised the God of heaven and gave thanks to him for his faithfulness and goodness to them.

Over the passage of time, Sarah died. Abraham purchased a field from the sons of Heth, who were Hivites, and buried her there.

Isaac grew to become a man. God once again faithfully blessed Isaac with a wife of Abraham's kindred, named Rebekah. Abraham even lived to see his two grandchildren, Esau and Jacob.

Finally the fateful day came in which Abraham died and was to be buried.

"Hello, little brother," Ishmael said as he beheld the last son of Abraham.

"Hello, Ishmael. I wish we could have met under better circumstances."

"What do you mean 'met'? I still remember bouncing you on my knee!"

Isaac smiled. "Too bad we couldn't have grown up together?"

"No," Ishmael said. "God is faithful and he had a plan for me and a plan for you. God has blessed me more than I ever deserved; but the promised one is going to come through you."

"You don't mind that the promise is coming through me and not you?"

Ishmael smiled. "No, not at all. I'm just glad to be part of this family. I'm thankful for the memories I had with our father and I'm glad to be able to see you again."

Together the sons of Abraham buried their father in the cave of Machpelah, beside his wife Sarah. When they were finished, they embraced each other and went their separate ways, without any knowledge of the shared destiny and fate of their children.

Chapter Twelve

"As it is written, Jacob have I loved, but Esau have I
hated."
Romans 9:13

1730 B.C.: Hebron

His conscience was killing him. While he slew the goats, and the whole time he was stirring the pot, a battle was commencing in his mind.

He sold me his birthright. He knows it and God knows it! I'm just taking what's clearly mine to begin with!

This would go on for a while, and then the other side would speak up.

If the line is going to come through you, and if you're to get the inheritance, then just trust God for it! Let him take care of it for you. What are you doing? This is your brother you're swindling!

About the time that this began to win over Jacob, his mother interrupted.

"Now Jacob, listen to me. I've told you this before and I'll tell you again: God told me that your brother was going to serve you, and that you were going to rule over him. The seed is supposed to come through you."

Jacob held up his hand. "So we're just helping God along on it?"

His mother was annoyed, but spoke in a hushed tone. "Look, your father is old and weary and has a hard time making decisions. And I'm sorry to say this, but right now he favors Esau simply because he loves the food he brings him. It's obvious that your father is thinking with his stomach and not listening to God. I know the line is supposed to be through you. God told me! But your father just hasn't gotten it! We have to do this or a terrible mistake will be made."

"I suppose you're right, Mother. I suppose you're right," Jacob said as he strapped the goat skins to his arms.

"Absolutely I'm right, young man. Sometimes God needs us to go out there and take what he has for us."

"By deception?"

Rebekah hesitated for a moment. "Look son, it's an imperfect world we live in and sometimes we have to make imperfect decisions. You can't look at what you're doing now. You have to look at where this is all going to go one day. The promise is yours, son. Go and take it!"

Jacob turned and walked into the room where his father lay. The man who as a young man willingly laid down his life in obedience to his father had gone the way of all flesh. He was an old man now, blind and hard of hearing.

"Esau, my boy! Are you back already?"

Jacob tried to sound jovial. "I am and you're going to love what I have for you today!"

"You sound a little funny, son. Are you feeling all right?"

Jacob winced and thought about sending up a prayer. "Not really, I, uh, haven't felt so good today—"

Isaac interrupted with a laugh, "Oh stop whining and give me the venison. You're starting to sound like your brother!"

Jacob flushed and tried to fake a laugh. "Well, here it is! Can I receive my blessing now?"

"Hold on, boy! It's like my father used to say, never give a blessing out on an empty stomach!"

"Did he really say that?"

"I don't know, son. I can't even remember what your mother said yesterday! How am I supposed to tell?"

Jacob laughed, but he felt terrible as he listened to his father joke around with his son who he thought was Esau. He knew that Isaac would be completely disgusted with him if he knew who was really in the room with him. Shame quickly turned to anxiety when his mother stuck her head in and quickly whispered, "Your brother is on his way back . . . right now!"

A bead of sweat formed on Jacob's forehead as he turned back to face his father. Isaac was still elaborating on the humorous conditions of old age and the fond memories of yesteryear. Jacob's nerves were fraying by the second.

"Why, there was this one time when your grandfather and I were hunting a deer and the thing led us all over the place!"

"Uh, I'm tired, you know, from the hunt —"

Still feeling rambunctious, Isaac interrupted, "You're tired from that hunt? You must have practically shot the animal from the front door you came back so quick!"

Jacob panicked as he heard his brother's tell-tale victory song drift into the tent. That was the song he sang whenever he was in a good mood and coming back from killing something. It usually meant everyone was going to enjoy a great meal; but instead of Jacob's mouth watering, he felt like his heart was going to beat out of his chest.

Isaac continued. "It still doesn't quite make sense to me! How'd you get back here so quickly?"

Jacob overheard his brother talking to his mother outside, telling her the story of how he tracked and killed the deer. Jacob winced at his brother's loud and boisterous storytelling.

"What's that I hear? What's that racket out there?" Isaac asked.

"Oh nothing. It must be Jacob and mother. I'm really hungry; would you please give me my blessing so that I can eat as well?"

"All right my boy, all right," Isaac smiled as he set the plate of food aside. "Give your father a kiss and tell him you love him."

"I love you, Father," Jacob said as he leaned forward to kiss his father's head.

Isaac breathed in the smell of Esau's garment and was fully convinced that he was speaking to his oldest son.

"See, the smell of my son is as the smell of a field which the LORD hath blessed. Therefore God give thee of the dew of heaven, and the fatness of the earth, and plenty of corn and wine: Let people serve thee, and nations bow down to thee. Be lord over thy brethren, and let thy mother's sons bow down to thee: cursed be every one that curseth thee, and blessed be he that blesseth thee."

"Thank you, Father," Jacob said as he scooted out the back while Esau stepped in the front.

"Hi Father! I have your food ready for you!"

"What? Who are you?" Isaac said surprised.

The firstborn was still jolly and unaware of what was going on. "Who am I? I'm your boy Esau! I've got the best deer meat you've ever tasted right her for you—"

Esau stopped and stared.   His father was trembling.

"Are you okay, Father? What's the matter?"

Isaac quivered, knowing that God had overruled what he wanted. "He's taken it. He has the blessing. There's nothing left for you. I'm sorry! I'm so sorry, son!"

Esau set the food down and rushed to his father's side to embrace him. "What are you talking about? Who took the blessing?"

"Jacob took it!"

"What?"

"Jacob took the blessing I meant for you! He tricked me; he said he was you! I didn't know, my son. I didn't know!"

Esau let out a bone-shaking and bitter cry of frustration. "No! No! Not again! How could he do this to me? You named him right when you called him Jacob! He's supplanted me twice now!"

Esau steadied his rage. "Do you have a blessing for me, Father? Anything at all?"

"I made him your lord and you're to serve him. I've promised him corn and wine. What is left for you?"

Esau was holding his father's shoulders now, crying. "There has to be something, anything. Please bless me, please!"

Isaac reached up and held Esau's wrist. "Behold, thy dwelling shall be the fatness of the earth, and of the dew of heaven from above; And by thy sword shalt thou live, and shalt serve thy brother; and it shall come to pass when thou shalt have the dominion, that thou shalt break his yoke from off thy neck."

Esau sat quietly for a moment and then spoke. "Thank-you, Father. Thank-you."

Rising up, Esau walked out of his father's bedroom and into the main room where he saw Jacob sitting next to his mother. The anger rose within him as he prepared himself a meal and sat down across from his brother. Their eyes met and Esau burned a hole right through Jacob.

The younger brother had the birthright and the blessing now, but he wondered at what cost.

Chapter Thirteen

"And he was afraid, and said, How dreadful *is* this place! this *is* none other but the house of God, and this *is* the gate of heaven."
Genesis 28:17

The Next Day: Hebron

"You have to leave, son. God told me you have to leave," Rebekah said with a sense of urgency in her voice.

Jacob felt a touch of agitation. "Things haven't been so good with me and Esau since last time I listened to you tell me what God told you."

"I know. We probably should have handled that differently."

Jacob didn't reply. He just looked at his mother.

"He's going to kill you, Jacob," she said. "You have to believe me on this. He's going to wait until your father dies, and then he's going to kill you. You need to leave for a little while until he calms down."

Jacob took his mother's words seriously and consulted with his father, who told him the best thing he could do was head to Padan-aram.

"Arise, go to Padanaram, to the house of Bethuel thy mother's father; and take thee a wife from thence of the daughters of Laban thy mother's brother. And God Almighty bless thee, and make thee fruitful, and multiply thee, that thou mayest be a multitude of people; and give thee the blessing of Abraham, to thee, and to thy seed with thee; that thou mayest inherit the land wherein thou art a stranger, which God gave unto Abraham."

With that Jacob hugged his parents goodbye and headed east with a walking stick in one hand and a sack over his shoulder. What he originally thought would only be a few days turned out to be twenty years away from his family. Having taken matters into his own hands, he would suffer the consequences of never seeing his mother again.

Out into the desert he went, filled with the fear of his brother's wrath to push him along. Tying a rag about his mouth and protecting his eyes from the sandy wind, he moved along one step in front of the other. Many times he wondered if this is what Ishmael and his mother must have felt like, being forced to leave the family. Jacob carried with him the promise of the seed, but his mind was on more immediate things such as food and water.

That evening the moon washed the desert floor with a pale blue light. Jacob worked quickly to prepare something to sleep by, moving rocks and stones into place to support his head as a pillow. He fell asleep quickly that night being weary from the journey of the day.

While he slept, he dreamed a dream from the LORD. Several angels walked right past where he was and looked to the sky. A golden ladder materialized and they began to climb it. On the flip side of the ladder, Jacob could see that there were angels using it to climb down.

Gazing up to the top of the ladder, Jacob saw a figure clothed in brightness. He was unable to make him out, but he knew it was the LORD.

"I am the LORD God of Abraham thy father, and the God of Isaac: the land whereon thou liest, to thee will I give it, and to thy seed; and thy seed shall be as the dust of the earth, and thou shalt spread abroad to the west, and to the east, and to the north, and to the south: and in thee and in thy seed shall all the families of the earth be blessed. And, behold, I am with thee, and will keep thee in all places whither thou goest, and will bring thee again into this land; for I will not leave thee, until I have done that which I have spoken to thee."

Jacob awoke with a start and realized that God had confirmed it. The promise was Jacob's and the seed would come through him. God had also promised Jacob that regardless of what would come up in his life, that he would be there with him.

Standing there, he was overwhelmed by the goodness and faithfulness of God, and another feeling began to come over Jacob. A chill ran up his spine as he realized he was receiving a vision in the same place that his grandfather had returned to when he left the land of Egypt. There was something powerful about this place.

Jacob rushed to gather up stones again, only this time to worship God, not to go to sleep. "This is the very gate of heaven," he said to himself.

Bowing before the altar, he prayed and poured oil on the stones. "LORD, if you will take care of me and bring me back home again one day, then you will always be my God, and I will always give back to you a tenth of what you give to me. This place will be the house of God."

Jacob changed the name of the place from Luz to Bethel, the house of God.

Chapter Fourteen

"Yea, he had power over the angel, and prevailed: he wept, and made supplication unto him: he found him *in* Bethel, and there he spake with us;"
Hosea 12:4

1710 B.C.: Peniel

T he inevitable was bound to happen and Jacob knew it. Twenty years had passed since that difficult day that Jacob was compelled to leave home, and now he was on his journey back with his family following. He knew sooner or later he was going to have a confrontation with his brother on his return to Hebron. He was bound to pass through the land of Edom, which was Esau's territory. Amazingly, the morning Jacob sent messengers out ahead of him, he saw angels and tried to take comfort in that. He knew God was there with him, but even that knowledge brought little. He was terrified that his brother was going to kill him.

The day came and went and the next morning Jacob watched the trail of dust kick up behind the two riders heading towards him. They were the messengers he sent out, and Jacob trembled when he considered the possibilities of what they had to say.

"He's on his way," the first man said as he slid off the horse. "Your brother is coming here with four hundred men."

Jacob was terrified. "Four hundred?"

"That's right. It's a regular army he's got out there and they're headed straight for us."

Staggering at the news, Jacob placed his hand on his forehead and tried to maintain his composure. "Okay, we have to do something; I have no idea what to do. We're all going to die, we're all going to die, Esau is going to—"

"What do you want us to do, Jacob?" the men asked.

Jacob snapped out of his state of panic for a moment and feigned courage. "I don't know yet, but I'll come up with something though. We're going to be okay."

The men rode away, wondering why they ever hired on.

Jacob watched them ride off and took a deep breath. Nervously, he began pacing back and forth, frantically wringing his hands.

"Oh God, help me, please help me, LORD. LORD, you told me to go home to my family and that's what I'm doing. I don't deserve any mercy from you and yet you've blessed me so much."

Jacob paused, took another deep breath and closed his eyes. "Please deliver me, LORD, from the hand of my brother. He's coming to kill me; he's coming to kill the child with the mother. LORD, please, you said you would do good unto me; and I know I don't deserve it, but please remember your promise unto me."

After praying a prayer of faith reminiscent of his grandfather, he immediately slipped back into the conniving pattern of the supplanter that he was. Jacob's ever-shrewd mind began scheming of ways to save his own skin.

Esau is a sucker for stuff. He always falls for immediate gratification, just like with the pottage. My best chance of escaping this ordeal is to overload him with gifts. He's always thinking about his stomach and what he wants. That will get him.

Jacob told his men to prepare wave after wave of presents to meet Esau on his way. Hundreds of animals would be given in attempt to appease the wrath of his brother. He sent them out in the afternoon ahead of himself, and that evening he kneeled alone in the darkness, praying and searching for guidance.

"What is thy name?" a figure suddenly said, standing about fifteen feet away from Jacob.

Jacob gasped when he saw him. It was the same person standing atop the ladder, back in Bethel. It was God himself, who had taken upon him the appearance of an angel. It was the angel of the LORD.

The angel smiled. "Are you going to answer me, or not?"

Jacob, still on his knees, cried out. "LORD, you have to help me; Esau is coming to kill me and my family. You have to do something!"

"I have to do something?" the angel laughed. "You've put yourself into this mess; let's see you bring yourself out of it."

With that, he turned his back to Jacob and began to walk away. Jacob scrambled to his feet and ran after the angel, tackling him by the waist. As if he was genuinely surprised by this and never saw it coming, the angel grunted and fell to the ground with Jacob holding onto him.

"Be gone," the angel said as he stood up and tossed Jacob to the side like a child's plaything. He then resumed his stroll away from the desperate man.

"No, you can't go!" Jacob screamed as he hurled himself again at the angel. The angel of the LORD simply stepped to the side and gave Jacob a little shove. Jacob fell to the ground again, and again he stood up.

The angel faced him. "Give me your name."

Jacob was bent over, holding his side. "LORD, please help me. What about your promise to never leave me?"

"Perhaps I shall stand by your side as he slays you."

"But you said that you'd multiply my seed as the—"

"And I will," the LORD said, finishing his sentence. "You already have several sons; you don't need to be around any longer for me to fulfill that one."

Jacob and the angel stared at each other. He grabbed the LORD's wrists, but God kicked him off again. He scrambled to his feet and jumped on the LORD's back. He squirmed and wiggled as the angel grasped for him. Finally the angel pulled him off by his arm and slammed him to the ground. Then Jacob kicked the LORD's feet out from under him and brought him down too. They wrestled and grappled and kicked and clawed like this for hours. Where Jacob had blood, sweat and dirt in his eyes, the LORD just chuckled and played along. Finally Jacob found himself exhausted, sitting on the ground with his back to a tree.

"Well," the angel said as he turned to walk away, "I guess I'll be seeing you later then."

"No!" Jacob screamed as he ran after him. The LORD spun and clotheslined him across the chest, laying him out flat on his back. Smiling, he bent over and looked at Jacob who was gasping to catch his breath.

"I'll give you this," the LORD said, "your brother quit a lot sooner than you. He cried for about an hour and gave up. We're halfway through the night now, and you're still going strong."

Jacob rolled over and grabbed the LORD's leg like a little child, sitting on his foot.

"You can't go until you bless me!"

This was about all the angel could handle. Looking down at the man, he crossed his arms and laughed. The angel of the LORD chuckled as he tried to kick the poor man off his leg. Jacob held on, with his face rubbing up against the angel's kneecap.

Jacob was stubborn, to say the least. "I'm going to die tomorrow and you're laughing! I need a blessing! I must have a blessing!"

"I've noticed you're really good at figuring out ways of getting blessings, aren't you?"

Jacob paused, but didn't reply.

"You always find a way to put yourself in and out of trouble, don't you? You're always running from some mess you created and that clever mind of yours somehow figures a way out."

Jacob still didn't respond.

"All right," God said bending over. "I'll be seeing you later."

With that, the Almighty tapped Jacob's hip with his finger. "Let's see you run now, boy."

Something snapped within Jacob's leg. He let go, screaming in pain and rolling in the dirt. The crippling pain shot through his bones, enough to cause a less determined man to pass out.

All the while Jacob was writhing in pain, the angel was walking away. He stopped about twenty feet away and looked at Jacob. He watched as Jacob crawled to him on his belly, dragging his limp leg behind him.

"Don't go, please," Jacob said as he grabbed the angel's foot.

"Let go, I have to leave. Daylight is coming."

"Please stay."

"No. Let go."

They stayed there for another hour and neither one spoke a word. A combination of the pain in his leg, his survival instinct, and the desire for a blessing kept Jacob awake.

The angel spoke first. "Okay, time's up. Let go of me."

"I need a blessing. I must have a blessing," Jacob whimpered.

"Speak your name," the LORD replied.

At that moment, a vision flashed before the mind of Jacob. He saw a young man manipulating his brother to take something from him. Then he was standing before his blind father, who, like the angel, was asking him what his name was. He saw himself swindling his uncle. Jacob at last had seen who and what he truly was.

Finally broken, Jacob sobbed the words. "I'm Jacob! I'm the supplanter! I'm a liar and a cheat; outside of you there's nothing good about me. I deserve to die, and, if that's what you want, then that's what I'll get. My name is Jacob!"

In compassion the LORD bent over and picked up the brokenhearted man from under his arms and held him out in front of him like a little child. "Not anymore it's not. Your name is no longer Jacob. It's Israel. For as a prince hast thou power with God and man and hast prevailed."

Setting him upon his feet the LORD continued. "Without me, there isn't any way you could stand there right now. I'm going to let you live and I'm going to let you walk; but to remind you of what leaning upon your own understanding will do for you, I'm also going to let you limp the rest of your life.

"Goodbye, Israel!"

The angel of the LORD turned to leave and surprisingly Israel wasn't finished yet. "Tell me, I pray thee, thy name."

The LORD smiled and turned back to him, "Why do you ask what my name is? You know who I am. In spite of all the trouble you find yourself in, Israel, you are blessed because you desire that which is of me.

"Even after this night is over with and even though your life has been spared and you've received your blessing, you still don't want me to leave. You still have a few more lessons to learn, but you're going to be just fine."

And with that, the angel of the LORD disappeared.

Jacob called the place where he wrestled with the angel, Peniel, which means God's face.

The next day Israel met his brother. Esau ran to him and gave him a bear hug that took his breath away.

"What's with all these things you keep sending me, little brother? I have enough stuff as it is. God has blessed me greatly, and I don't need anymore!"

Israel was relieved to see that not only did his brother not want to kill him, but that he was actually happy to see him.

"Oh please take it all," Israel said. "If I find any grace in your sight, just take it, brother."

"Okay, sure, whatever you want Jake," Esau laughed.

The two brothers spent the day together laughing and telling stories. Esau was overjoyed to meet Israel's wives and children. Israel listened as Esau related his side of the story and what had happened to him over the last twenty years.

God had humbled Esau as well and showed him his need for reliance on the LORD. All the while Israel was scheming and running, God was also working in the heart of Esau; breaking him down, humbling him, teaching him what forgiveness was.

Apparently the LORD wasn't just the God of Abraham, Isaac and Israel; he was also the God of Abraham, Isaac and Esau.

But the promise belonged to Israel.

Chapter Fifteen

**"Moreover he refused the tabernacle of Joseph, and
chose not the tribe of Ephraim:"**
Ps. 78:67

1660 B.C.: Hebron

The final chapter on Israel's life came to a close much like his own father's, with his sons meeting together. And while they were gathering around the bed of the old patriarch, waiting to hear his last will and testament, a conversation was taking place between two powerful beings in the third heaven.

"Who do you think he'll pick?" Gabriel said to Michael as they looked upon the scene and watched it transpire.

"It's hard to tell, but I don't think for a second that it will be Reuben."

"I agree. The firstborn hasn't received it yet, and I don't see why that would change now, especially when you consider what that firstborn did."

Laying upon his bed, the old man lifted up his wavering hand and began to speak. "Reuben, thou art my firstborn, my might, and the beginning of my strength, the excellency of dignity, and the excellency of power: unstable as water, thou shalt not excel; because thou wentest up to thy father's bed; then defiledst thou it. He went up to my couch."

"You saw that one coming," Gabriel said. "But that still doesn't answer my question: who is Israel going to pick? Who do you think God is going to use to bring the seed into the world?"

"I'd say Joseph," Michael said. "It makes the most sense. Out of the twelve of them, he's the only one that seems to have it together."

Gabriel smiled. "It's not going to be Joseph."

Michael was taken aback a little by this and tried to explain himself. "What do you mean it's not going to be Joseph? Without a doubt he's the one who resembles the Daysman the most."

"Absolutely, he does. But let me ask you this: would you trust the old Jacob over Esau? You couldn't turn your back on the man! Jacob was about as crooked as they come, but God chose him over Esau."

"Well, that's because Jacob's heart desired the right things," Michael said. "Esau was a good man, but he was carnally minded. He had no zeal for the

LORD, even though everyone would want him as a neighbor."

Gabriel nodded. "But that's only part of it; Jacob came to a point where he was willing to see himself for who he was. He saw the truth. He saw the truth and was willing to accept and submit to it."

Michael raised one eyebrow. "You might have a point there."

"Of course I do!" Gabriel laughed. "You military types are all the same, always looking for rank and position when it comes to these sorts of things. Face it: no one on Earth deserves the seed anymore than anyone else. Joseph may be the cleanest one of the group, but he hasn't earned anything. They're all a bunch of sinners that deserve Hell."

"Okay, well, who is it going to be then?" Michael said impatiently.

Gabriel smiled and pointed down to the scene as it was unfolding. "It's that one."

"Surely you jest. That one? He's probably the grimiest one out of all of them! He was the one who wanted to make a profit off his brother by selling him! He slept with his daughter-in-law thinking she was a whore! God is going to pick him over Joseph?"

"Joseph had pride and he lied about the cup," Gabriel responded.

"Well, that's not nearly as bad as what—"

"That one didn't lie, or make any excuses. When the woman accused him, he owned up to it. He could have lied; but not only did he admit to what he did, he also realized his own inadequacy and publically said the woman was more righteous than he."

"Hmmm," Michael said.

"Hmmm is right! Joseph had to spend years in jail before he started to show a little humility. He still battles that to this day. Joseph is a special one; but he's proud sometimes, and God resisteth the proud!"

While Gabriel was talking in the mind of Michael the archangel, a memory was unveiling itself. It was one of the most dramatic moments in the lives of the sons of Israel:

Joseph stood before his brothers; his heart in his throat the entire time he spoke. He had been deceiving his brothers in not revealing his true identity to them. In their eyes he was the second in charge of all of Egypt. He was also the one that was going to decide whether or not Benjamin would live free or die a slave. Just when the brothers thought they were in the clear, the silver cup had been found in Benjamin's bag; and now they all stood condemned before Joseph.

They listened to Joseph speak in Egyptian and in anticipation they hung on every word of the translation. Then one of the men took a step forward and away from the others and beseeched the ruler for Benjamin's sake.

"What can we say? What can we do to save his life? How can we clear ourselves? God hath found the iniquity of thy servants. We're all guilty here, but Benjamin didn't do anything. Please let him go!"

Joseph looked upon his brother. Years ago the one he saw before him had no problem with killing him, but thanks to Reuben he didn't have the chance to do so. That didn't stop him for long. Instead of killing Joseph, he simply sold him into slavery.

When Joseph pondered the words and the spirit of his older brother he recognized that something had come over him. There was a change in this man that stood before him. Joseph's heart began to soften and his will wavered.

"It's not up for discussion! Benjamin stays! He will be my servant. He stole the cup; he's mine. I have no concern for the rest of you; you may depart in peace and go back to your father."

The older brother wouldn't take no for an answer. "Please hear me! Please do not be angry with me."

He took a few more steps towards him and continued. "You asked before if we have a father. We do. He's an old man, gray and feeble. We told him we would come here for food, and we told him about this whole mess and about how you needed to meet Benjamin."

His brother's eyes were breaking Joseph's heart with every step. "My father didn't want us to take Benjamin because he's very near and dear to him. He had another son once and our father believes that he was killed by a wild animal. I've seen the pain and hurt that has come over my father since that day, and I know it's my fault. I take the blame.

"There isn't any way that I can allow that to happen again."

Judah stopped and fell to his knees before Joseph, bowing his head. "Take me. I'll take his place. I'm the one who deserves it. I'm the betrayer of innocent blood. I'm the guilty one. I'll take his place! I'll take his place. Let Benjamin free and take me instead!"

At that point Judah believed his life was doomed to slavery, separated from his brethren. He would never see his father again. He would never see his wife again. His life would be wasted as a slave. There was no attempt to bargain or make an excuse to save his own skin. When he could have gone free, by his own volition, Judah kneeled and accepted his fate in order to save another.

His heart could not sink any lower than it was. But in heaven, coronation music was loudly sounding. God placed a crown upon the contrite head of Judah that day and swore that from his line the Messiah would come.

The memory faded as quickly as it had come. Michael and Gabriel both looked down over the banisters of heaven just in time to watch as the old patriarch breathed the words.

"The scepter shall not depart from Judah, nor a lawgiver from between his feet, until Shiloh come; and unto him shall the gathering of the people be."

When Jacob had made an end of commanding his sons he gathered up his feet into the bed and yielded up the ghost, and was gathered unto his people.

And Joseph fell upon his father's face and wept upon him and kissed him.

Another great patriarch had died and his sons grew old in the land of Egypt, far away from the

Promised Land given to their father Abraham. Joseph's brothers feared that with Jacob gone, he would turn on them. Joseph, never ceasing to be an example of graciousness and forgiveness, quickly put these fears to rest.

In due course the time came when Joseph, the great picture of the coming king, would die and be gathered unto his people just as Jacob had been. With the promise of the kingdom ever ringing in their hearts, his remaining brothers and children came to hear the lasts words of the great prophet.

His voice was weak and quivering. "I'm dying now, boys," he said as he looked to grandchildren. "I won't be here for you anymore. You're going to have to know the LORD without me now. If you seek him, he'll visit you as he always has our family."

Joseph's hand reached out and rested on Benjamin's. "I'm going to see our father soon."

The old man coughed and grunted as he tried to sit up. His sons, Ephraim and Manasseh, helped him straighten to his full height. With his last dying words, his eyes flashed with renewed strength.

"I'm dying, but the promise lives on. God will surely visit you and when he does, he's going to take you out of this land and bring you into the land which he sware to Abraham, to Isaac and to Jacob."

Joseph paused and then cracked a smile. "And when he does, you make sure to take my dusty old bones out of here and bury them where they belong."

Chapter Sixteen

"The thing that hath been, it *is that* which shall be;
and that which is done *is* that which shall be done:
and *there is* no new *thing* under the sun."
Ecclesiastes 1:9

1542 B.C.: The Backside of Jupiter

The adversary was at work. Not content to simply allow the people of God to grow into a mighty nation within the country of Egypt, Satan had devised a plan to keep them there and destroy the messianic line. It had been over ninety years since Joseph had died and the people had missed their opportunity to leave the land of Goshen and go back to the Promised Land of Abraham, Isaac and Jacob.

"I have called this meeting to outline the final phase of my plan to prevent the seed of the woman," Satan said as he stood before the mass of dark and twisted beings.

"But before we go any further, Wormwood is going to take you back to how we came to this point."

The fallen angel Wormwood took center stage and began to speak. "When Israel could have left Egypt, we delayed them. When they could have gone back to the land of their forefathers, we made them comfortable."

A hush fell over the crowd. "The sin of Sodom has become the sin of Israel. As we all know, the final destructive phase of those people was sexual perversion, but I'd like to draw your attention to what eventually brought them to that point.

"The sin of Sodom was pride, fullness of bread and abundance of idleness. Neither did she strengthen the hand of the poor and needy. It was complacency that brought her down and it is complacency that has kept Israel right where we want her."

The crowd cheered and Wormwood held up his hand to quiet them. "We also understand all too well that men are much more apt to agree to something with a full belly than an empty heart. With that principle in mind, our servants in Egypt began removing the freedoms of the Israelites bit by bit. This was best done in the name of providing protection from Egypt and Israel's enemies and of course providing for the basic needs of the people."

Wormwood smiled. "The king of Egypt has replaced the God of Israel as the great provider, protector and educator of the people!"

The crowd roared with laughter and cheers. "Once the king has become the provider, he has by default become something akin to a god to them. Quite naturally, a god that protects and provides for his people has every right to tell them what is right and wrong, what to do and what not to do, and of course who to marry and who not to.

"God's people have gone to their proxy god and have begun to take on his ideologies and morality. Their children have been educated by our people and now they are marrying them. Israel has begun to intermingle and integrate its dress, music and culture with ours."

The demons and devils all stood nodding their heads and whispering one to another. Wormwood laughed as he went on.

"Don't worry! This hasn't resulted in Satan's people becoming righteous all of a sudden! Do you realize that when God looks down on his people now he sees a group of individuals that have replaced him in every way? They are lazy and idle; they go to their rulers instead of God. They are unwilling to take the land God has for them because they are content with Goshen and best of all they have begun to worship the idols of the Egyptians! Can it get any better than this?"

Wormwood bowed and backed away as Satan stepped back into his place. Smiling, he looked back at Wormwood. "Of course it can!"

Silencing the crowd, Satan went on. "What happens next is simple: we make them suffer and then we kill them."

"I believe the people of God have enjoyed the blessings of freedom for far too long. They have grown accustomed to it and have multiplied and become nice and fat for the slaughter."

Satan paused and took in the view of his dark kingdom. "You all know me. I'm not a big fan of freedom in any way. What I like to do is convince a people that they are rich and increased with goods and have need of nothing; when in reality, they are wretched and miserable, and poor and blind and naked."

A smile came across his face. "And nobody does it better than I do it."

"We have the people of God in our land, relying upon our people and absorbing their culture, ideas, morals and gods. Even if God wanted to send them a deliverer, why would he bother? So he could rescue a morally and spiritually bankrupt people?

"The fact is, God's people are now our people. The hedge of protection is down, and we can do what we want with them. We'll start with slavery and finish with the eradication of all newborn males. With no men to lead, the women will be completely absorbed into Egypt. This will ensure that the line of Israel dies and with it the promise of the coming seed.

God is not going to bless a wicked people, and he is not going to save them either.

"Their lives are ours for the taking."

Chapter Seventeen

"For I *am* the LORD, I change not; therefore ye sons
of Jacob are not consumed."
Malachi 3:6

1463 B.C.: The Backside of the Desert

An old man walked across the desert
floor, humbly watching the sheep that
belonged to his wife's father.   One

would never imagine that this man had been taught by the sharpest minds in the world and educated by the most prestigious teachers of Egypt. Nothing about him declared his background of royalty within the house of Pharaoh, or that he was a prince of the most powerful nation in the world.

There were many things to know about this man. He was a murderer, and he was a failure. He was the Jewish boy, who as a baby, was rescued by a princess of Egypt and raised in luxury. Forty years ago, in a foolish act of violence, he had killed an Egyptian whom he had spied persecuting one of his Hebrew brethren. He had hoped to use his royal standing within the house of Egypt to put an end to the suffering of his people, but the rash action he took that day turned him into a fugitive. His efforts had failed a long time ago, and now here he was in the backside of the desert scratching out a meager existence with what few remaining years he had left.

Moses thought he was at the end of his life, but he had no idea what lay before him.

He wiped the perspiration from his face with a cloth and squinted to see the flame on the horizon. He was amazed to see that the brushfire wasn't spreading and didn't burn itself out. His curiosity overcame him, and he decided to take a look.

Moses stared in disbelief as he saw the bush continue to burn without stopping. After ten minutes, it hadn't even begun to slow down. His bewilderment was suddenly interrupted by a booming voice that came straight from the bush.

"Moses, Moses."

Moses knew it could be no one else other than the LORD.

"Here am I," Moses said.

"Draw not nigh hither: put off thy shoes from off thy feet, for the place whereon thou standest is holy ground."

While Moses quickly and nervously removed his shoes, the LORD continued. "I am the God of Abraham, Isaac and Jacob."

Moses was terrified. He lay prostrate on the ground before the bush, with his hands covering his face.

"I have seen the affliction of my people Israel at the hand of the Egyptians, The LORD said. "I have heard their cry and know their sorrow. As this bush goes through the fire and never burns up, so are my people Israel. They have suffered and will suffer, but because of my promise they will never be consumed. They failed to deserve deliverance, but my promise to Abraham still stands."

The LORD continued. "I have come down to free them and to bring them into a land flowing with milk and honey. You will be a prophet and king unto them. You will bring them out of Egypt into the Promised Land once you have spoken to Pharoah."

Moses had mixed feelings about this whole thing. He wanted to see Israel delivered, but he didn't want to be the one in charge of the whole process. He knew what the Egyptians were like and more importantly he knew what the Hebrews were like. If there were ever a people that didn't deserve to be saved, it was the Israelites. Moses did not relish the idea of confronting the cruel Egyptians to try and save a people that he knew would not cooperate.

"Who am I LORD, to speak to Pharaoh or to bring Israel out of Egypt?"

"Surely I will be with thee."

Moses brought about a second objection. "Well, when I speak to the Israelites, they will want to know what your name is. What should I tell them?"

"I AM THAT I AM. Tell them that I AM hath sent thee."

Moses' mind raced for another reason not to become involved, and the LORD continued to speak.

"Go and gather the elders of the children of Israel and tell them that I will bring them into the land of the Canaanites, and the Hittites, and the Amorites, and the Perizzites, and the Hivites, and the Jebusites; for they are an abomination unto me and I gave them space to repent but they would not. Also, I am sure the king of Egypt will not let you go, no, not by a mighty hand."

While the LORD spoke, Moses arose and dusted himself off. "LORD, they won't believe me. You know those people better than I do. They will say that you never appeared unto me."

"What is that in thine hand?"

Moses blinked and looked down. "It's a rod, LORD."

"Throw it on the ground."

Bewildered, Moses dropped the rod, and it immediately turned into a snake that snapped at his bare foot, missing it by inches. Moses screamed and fled from the snake.

"Moses, you're not going to go anywhere unless you learn to face your fears. Turn around and grab the snake."

Moses reasoned that he was in a win-win situation. If the snake killed him, he wouldn't have to confront Pharaoh. If the LORD saved his life here, then at least he'd still be alive. Lastly, he figured he really didn't have any other option other than to obey.

Moses spun around and faced the snake as it sprung for his leg again. He snapped it out of the air and it hardened back into a rod.

"We're not done yet," the LORD said. "Put your hand into your bosom."

Moses slipped his hand into his robe and took it out. He was horrified to see that it had turned leprous.

"Put it back in again," the LORD said.

Moses obeyed and when he pulled his hand back out it had turned back to normal.

"Moses," the LORD said, "did you ever notice that Abraham, Isaac and Jacob never had problems with diseases?"

"I never thought about that LORD," Moses said as he was still trying to mentally absorb what had just happened.

"Well, they never did. Neither did any of their children. In fact, you Hebrews never had any problems with sickness until you went down to Egypt."

Moses mind raced as he tried to ponder this thought.

"I have promised the children of Israel a physical and earthly kingdom with physical and earthly blessings. If they diligently hearken unto my voice and do that which is right in my sight, they won't have to worry about diseases any more."

The LORD went on. "I want you to show these signs unto the elders and if they still don't believe you, take some water out of the river and pour it on the ground in front of them. It will turn into blood once it hits the dirt."

Moses pondered this and the LORD continued. "You are made up of water Moses, but the life of the flesh is in the blood. The ground is cursed and so is your blood."

Moses found another reason not to obey. "LORD, I'm not a good speaker. I become nervous at times. I stutter when I'm nervous, and I'm not very eloquent. I think it would be better if you found someone else for this job."

"You stutter when you're nervous?" the LORD said, as if surprised. "That's interesting because I haven't heard you stutter yet. You must not be nervous when you're talking with me."

Moses gasped. "Oh no! I'm terrified to speak to you. I abhor myself in dust and ashes!"

"But yet you still haven't stuttered one time. With everything you've seen, Moses, don't you think that I can be with your mouth? Who made man's mouth? Have not I, the LORD?"

Completely cornered in the conversation, Moses found his fifth and final protest. "LORD, please just use someone else. Please."

This made the LORD angry. "If I wanted someone else I would have picked someone else, Moses. But if it is any comfort unto you, I have sent Aaron unto you to help you. He'll be your spokesman and for better and worse your right-hand man. This is not what I wanted, but I understand that you are but flesh and blood. Now go into Egypt, and Aaron will meet you on the way. Those that sought your life are all dead now."

"Yes LORD," Moses said, realizing that regardless of whatever excuse he came up with, the call of God was without repentance and that it would haunt him forever unless he yielded.

"One other thing, Moses," the LORD said.

"Yes, LORD?"

"Don't forget your rod."

Chapter Eighteen

"Fear ye not, neither be afraid: have not I told thee
from that time, and have declared *it?* ye *are* even my
witnesses. Is there a God beside me? yea, *there is* no
God; I know not *any.*"

Isaiah 44:8

1462 B.C.: The Shoreline of the Red Sea

Moses could taste the salt in the air. He stood elevated above all the refugees of the seed of Abraham. He had the rod of God in his hand and a lump in his throat the size of the Red Sea which lay behind him. He could see the dust cloud of Pharaoh and his chariots drawing near at an extremely uncomfortable rate. Panic was growing within the multitude and things were moving faster than Moses' senses would allow.

What Moses couldn't see was the Prince of Israel, Michael the Archangel, standing no less than five feet above him. Behind Michael was an angelic legion clad in golden armor. They stood with swords outstretched, ready to defend the people of God. Ra and Horus, Nut and Hathor, Isis, Sunu, Apis and all of the other supernatural princes of Egypt had been offended by the plagues and their armies rolled like a flood over the desert wasteland.

The heavens rumbled as the pillar of smoke and darkness appeared once again to block the path of the enemy. At night this cloud barricaded the Egyptians as an impenetrable wall of fire.

Shouts were heard among the people. "We can't stay here forever, Moses! They're going to figure out a way around the cloud sooner or later and then we're done for!"

The people were losing hope and continued complaining. "Did you bring us all the way out here just to have us killed? Maybe if we just surrender, they'll let us return?"

Moses cried out to the people and down deep he was hoping that God would hear him too. "Fear ye not, stand still and see the salvation of the LORD! God will fight for you and ye shall hold your peace."

The chariots had begun to come around both sides of the cloud and were closing in. Pharoah's rash anger had given him the courage to bet his life that the dark cloud wasn't lethal, and it looked as if he were right.

Moses wasn't panicking, he was praying. The LORD spoke to his heart, "Why are you talking to me when you know what to do? Just tell the people to walk into the sea and divide it with your rod."

Moses hesitated to respond just long enough for him to hear the LORD joke, "You did bring your rod, right?"

Moses' rod. He had certainly learned by now not to leave that behind. Even though it was just another piece of wood on the outside, God kept using it in mysterious ways. This was the same rod that brought down darkness, thunder, hail and fire on Egypt; not to mention it was still full from having eaten Pharoah's pets. But this was the main event; and with the powers of darkness poised to annihilate the people of God there was no better moment than now.

Filled with faith, he faced the Red Sea and held out his rod. From the east a sudden and massive rush of wind swept over the water and silenced the people. Hands were raised to protect eyes from the sand and the unseen satanic army was swept away.

Pharaoh's army roared on in pursuit.

The water was divided and without much prompting at all the people began to move across the chasm. Two giant walls of water flanked them as they walked across the dry ground. Little boys and girls giggled as they watched the bewildered fish stare at them through the walls, and their parents urged them onwards.

God moved and the cloud turned to flame in front of the Egyptians. It once again moved to block their path. Unwilling and unable to charge straight into an obstacle of pulsing fire, the chariots continually maneuvered to try to find a way around.

This provided the children of Israel the time they needed to bring most of their people across.

Pharaoh's mind was irrational. His thoughts ricocheted between wondering if he was being toyed with by the God of Heaven and being too enraged to care. Barking orders at his soldiers, Pharaoh finally negotiated past the pillar of fire, charging headlong after the remnants that were just crossing the other side. Between the rantings of Pharaoh and the fury of the theophany behind them, the chariot captains pushed their horses too hard; and halfway across the wheels started breaking off.

Pharaoh was thrown out of his chariot when his driver lost control and it overturned. He lay with his face in the sand, bloodied and bruised, the heat of the sun weighing down on him. Pulling himself off the ground, he spit the salt from his lips and looked around to see the same scene being reenacted among all his troops. He knew what was coming, and his heart hardened as he saw it.

And at the end it was this man, who had been given ample opportunities to see the truth and obey the word of the LORD, who shook his fist at the heavens and cursed God while the walls of water came crashing down.

The gods and soldiers of Egypt had been defeated, and the people of the promise continued on toward the land of their father Abraham and the kingdom that awaited them. The dead bodies washed up on the shore as Israel danced and sang praises to the God of their deliverance.

As long as the people lived, the promise of the seed lived with them.

Chapter Nineteen

"He found him in a desert land, and in the waste
howling wilderness; he led him about, he instructed
him, he kept him as the apple of his eye."
Deuteronomy 32:10

1462 B.C.: Mount Sinai

In any ordinary situation it would be odd to see a man over eighty years trudge up the same mountain for the fifth time in a month, but things were hardly ever normal in Sinai. From the sky raining food, to a rock gushing water, God had blessed and provided for the Israelites in spite of their constant bickerings and murmurings whenever things didn't go just right.

The first battle for the Promised Land had already been waged, and the Amalekites had lost. The Israelites prevailed while Moses' weary arms were held up high in the air, as one who would be faithful unto death. The young warrior who showed himself strong that day, Joshua, was told that God would forever war against Amalek until he was put out of remembrance from under heaven.

The people came to Mount Sinai and it was there that God appeared again in thunders, lightnings and in a thick cloud. The people trembled and were afraid to even look, let alone approach the mount where God dwelt. Mount Sinai, also known as Mt. Horeb, was sanctified unto the LORD; and anyone or anything that touched it would certainly die. Except for Moses, who was actually told to climb it and to speak with Jehovah. The people agreed together that

God was much too fearsome to talk with, and they were all very happy that it was Moses' job to be the mediator. And so began the first of many times in which Moses, who was in great shape for a man his age, began his mountain-climbing profession.

This last time was very different, however. Aaron, Nadab, Abihu and seventy of the elders of Israel were allowed to come halfway up the mount and it was there that they literally saw the God of Israel upon his throne, high and lifted up. They were lost in the beauty and glory of God, and they praised him together that day. Moses was privileged to go further up the mountain when he was called of God, and Joshua came with him. The rest of the group descended back down to the people to wait for their return.

Throughout all of this process, things were becoming very clear for the people of Israel. God was giving them a directive to go into a specific area of the world and take it over. They were to establish and spread a kingdom, and if it were to be by military force then so be it. The peoples who inhabited the land belonging to Abraham were unrepentant and abhorrently wicked before the LORD. If they did not leave on their own then they would be wiped out.

However a conditional covenant was starting to take form between God and Israel. God promised to feed them and give them water to drink. In addition, he promised to prevent them from acquiring diseases, defeat their enemies, and by and large bless and protect them. On the other hand, the people were required to stay faithful unto God and to obey his law.

And it was at that point that the fifth cherub began to take note of the situation. Satan had seen how easily his armies were simply cast away at the Red Sea, and he was looking for a weakness by which to strike back. From what he had gathered, God wasn't giving them a free ride. They had to keep up their end of the bargain or they were on their own. Yes, God had made a promise to Abraham to give his descendents the land; and Satan knew there was nothing he could do about that, but at the same time God was also telling them now that if they forsook his way, they would perish in the land.

Satan pondered the opportunity that lay before him. If God were forced to destroy the people because of sin, would he in fact be breaking his own word to Abraham? What would happen then?

This possible quirk of fate both intrigued and perplexed the angel of light; and he assumed that he must be, absolutely had to be, missing something from this delicious equation. He decided that the best thing he could do was to push the people toward vileness in an effort to kill as many of them as he could. After all, beamed Satan, *who better to kill these people than the one who made them?*

Satan delved into work immediately after Moses had gone up the mount, and by now the darts were starting to take effect. He planted thoughts in their minds and the people welcomed them. *Why not take a break while Moses is gone? You deserve it after all. You've been through a lot.*

This thought, of course, led to a spirit of laziness and an abundance of idleness filled the congregation. Idleness turned to boredom for some and restlessness for others. The people grew discontent while the spirits of darkness continued their work.

Will this ever be over? When is Moses coming back, or is he coming back at all?

Quite naturally, of course, when the people grew discontent, they shared it with each other. Soon their rotten attitudes bred and spread like rabbits.

This is monotonous. Remember when life was fun? Back when you were in Egypt?

It was at that time that some musically talented, but spiritually deficient fool, decided that he would take it upon himself to bless everyone with a song from the old days. It started with him swaying and repeating it to himself. He grew louder and bolder the more people began to cheer. Instruments were quickly brought to bear, and a driving and intoxicating rhythm swept across the assembly. The people shouted and danced; unrighteous passions were unleashed and lewdness abounded.

Jehovah never gave you a good time like this: worship me.

And so they did. A spiritual darkness set across the people, and they decided that they no longer wanted to follow a God of law and liberty; they wanted a god of lust, anarchy and bondage. Rampant fornication and vileness was the method of worship and the god that arose was the golden calf. Tammuz, the son and incestuous husband of the wife of Nimrod, had returned with a vengeance. His name was Baal, and the worship service was in full swing.

Meanwhile up on the mount, God was laying out the law for Moses by which he expected Israel to operate. The commandments sounded off like thunder from the LORD, and they were burned into the stone tables with his finger. Joshua waited around the corner, hearing but not witnessing the splendor of the entire event.

"Moses," the LORD said, "get thee down, for thy people which you brought out of Egypt have corrupted themselves."

My people? Moses thought.

The LORD continued. "They have turned quickly out of the way in which I have commanded them and have turned unto a molten calf. They are worshipping it, sacrificing unto it, and praising it for bringing them out of the land of Egypt.

I have watched them, endured their constant complaining and murmuring, and have seen that they are a rebellious and stiffnecked people. I want you to go down to them and leave me for now; let me alone that my wrath may wax hot against them. I intend to consume them with the fire of my rage and when they are destroyed I'll start over with you."

The mountain shook and Moses' heart trembled while the voice of the LORD thundered of slaying this wicked nation and starting anew. It was then that the greatest defining moment of this patriarch's life was about to occur. Here stood the man who could not control his own anger and had slain an Egyptian, hiding him in the sand. This was the recluse who had hid in the desert from both his royal heritage and his Jewish ancestry, offering up every excuse he could to keep from delivering his own people. He wanted nothing to do with them. He didn't want to be a hero; he didn't want to save them. All he ever really wanted was to live by himself with his family and herd sheep.

At this golden moment in time, he found he had his opportunity to have everything he really wanted in the first place; the best part was that it was God's idea and not his. He was about to become the second Abraham. God was going to start the whole thing over with him.

"Don't do it, LORD. Please don't do it."

The man who stood now before the God of the Ages was not the same man who had shuffled along in the barren wasteland tending to his flock. Here stood a man of courage and devotion, with an unflinching loyalty to his God and a love for his people.

"Oh LORD my God, why are you angry with thy people that thou brought out of Egypt with great power and a mighty hand? Remember thine enemies, the Egyptians and know what they will say if you do this. Your name, LORD, will be mocked if these people die and it will seem as if you failed. Please remember your promise to Abraham, Isaac and Israel, and to their seed."

Moses' prayer spoke to God of his glory, faithfulness, integrity, and promises. It was respectful and reasonable. It was persuasive.

And it was answered; the LORD repented of the evil which he thought to do unto his people.

Moses thanked God and began his descent down the mount. Rounding the corner Joshua met him. "Moses, I think there's some kind of battle going on down there; I hear the sound of war coming from the camp!"

"That isn't war, Joshua. That is music you're hearing."

Moses stormed down the mountain like a hurricane with Joshua in the rear trying to keep up. Reaching the outskirts of the camp, he stood upon a rock, and it was there that his voice detonated like the sound of Enoch and Noah.

"You wicked and adulterous generation! You've rejected the God of your fathers, and you are worthy of death!"

The music stopped, the dancing trailed off. Everyone stood there with their mouths wide open.

Moses threw the stone tables, and they shattered at the base of the altar. He stormed over to the image, ripping a stone mallet out of the hand of a nearby goldsmith on the way. With a mighty swing he struck the image and broke off its head. He didn't let up; with strength not his own, Moses began pounding the golden calf and burned it in fire until it was reduced to powder. Then he commanded the terrified people to drink it in their water. While they choked the water down, he spun and put his finger on the chest of the high priest.

"How'd you ever let this happen, Aaron?"

This time it was Aaron who was slow of speech and stammered. "Don't be angry my lord . . ."

"Your lord?" Moses roared back. "Your LORD is Jehovah, and he came this close to roasting you and everyone else here! Now tell me what happened!"

"The people, well, you know they're bent on mischief, and well, they just gave me all their gold and I just happened to put it into the fire, and before you know it out came this calf."

Moses finished the story for him. "And then they took their clothes off and started worshipping a piece of metal? You just went up the mount with me and saw the glory of Jehovah with your own eyes, and yet you not only allowed this, but you also contributed!"

Moses paused and looked around. "Okay, who is on the LORD's side?"

A group of repentant sinners gathered themselves unto him.

Holding up the prophetic hand, Moses spoke. "Thus saith the LORD God of Israel, put every man his sword by his side and go in and out from gate to gate, throughout the camp, and slay every man his companion and every man his neighbor."

That day three thousand of the children of Israel were slain. Afterwards, Moses spoke to the people of justice and mercy and of consecration unto their God. He spoke to them from a broken heart. He told them that he was going to return to the mount for new tablets and to speak to God about making atonement for their sin.

What he didn't tell them, however, was that he himself was willing to be the atonement for their sin. Now it was hours later and he knelt before Jehovah, willing to sacrifice his soul to save the souls of the people.

"Oh, this people have sinned a great sin and have made them gods of gold. Yet LORD, please forgive them, but if you will not— then please LORD, blot me. Blot my name I pray, out of the book that thou hast written."

The LORD did not blot Moses' name out of the book and he allowed the children of Israel to survive. He did promise, however, that many more would suffer for what they had done and that they would be plagued for their sin.

And yet in spite of everything, the people lived on. God had every right to destroy them all; he could have started over again with Moses, but the kingdom would have been delayed by generations and the testimony of the promise would have been marred by death and destruction. That would have been exactly what Satan wanted.

But Satan didn't get what he wanted that day because of the courage and prayer of a lonely old man walking through the desert tending to his beloved sheep.

Chapter Twenty

"He hath not beheld iniquity in Jacob, neither hath
he seen perverseness in Israel: the LORD his God *is*
with him, and the shout of a king *is* among them."
Numbers 23:21

1423 B.C.: Mt. Peor

The ensign for the nation of Moab fluttered in the wind as its king and his royal guard looked towards the valley below them. There were tents everywhere; the nation of Israel filled the valley. Stalled by a lack of faith for forty years, they had wandered around in the barren wilderness wiping out everyone they had run into. Aaron had died, but Moses was nearly one hundred and twenty years old and in just as good shape as he was at eighty. Or even forty, for that matter.

But, of course, Balak, the king of Moab, didn't care about Moses' current health status nearly as much he cared about his people and their future well-being. Based upon what he saw this army of shepherds do to the Amorites and the Bashanites, he knew he had only two options: leave or die. It wasn't a matter of fighting to actually win, fighting was simply a formality. Right now, no one was going to beat Israel.

Balak was wallowing in his spirit of fear and self-pity when suddenly a thought struck him. This thought was so original, so absolutely brilliant, that Balak was surprised that he had actually come up with it on his own. Why, it was almost as if someone had whispered the very idea in his ear.

Fight fire with fire: go get Balaam the prophet and see what he can do.

Now Balaam was a good man, but his best days were behind him. He had been a fiery preacher back in his day, but he had cooled off a lot since then. Learning that very fine lesson that couth and polish led to bigger crowds and offerings, the old prophet had begun to dial back the intensity of his messages. After all, Balaam reasoned, what good does it do to give someone all of the truth if they're just going to choke on it? And besides all that, what is truth?

These thoughts struggled within the preacher quite often and while there were times that he spoke the word of the LORD, those days were becoming farther and farther apart.

At this particular moment though, Balaam wasn't considering any of this. He was at home taking an afternoon nap, when out of the middle of nowhere an obnoxious thumping on the door woke him up.

"Balaam, son of Beor! Are you in there? Open up!"

Opening the door, Balaam rubbed his face as he listened to the king's detachment ramble on about the terrible people from Egypt and how they were going to wipe them all out. Apparently the king of Moab thought a retired street preacher was going to stop the army of God somehow.

"We know," the men said, "that whoever you bless is blessed and whoever you curse is cursed. Now the king wants to curse those people so we can go out to war against them and win. Right now we don't stand a chance!"

It would seem that somewhere along the line the message had been lost and people had begun to think that it was Balaam who determined who was blessed and who was cursed. He didn't seem to mind and allowed the men to continue in their frightful tirade.

"The king has requested your presence to discuss this further. If we don't stop them, Balaam, then these people are going to cover the face of the entire Earth."

Balaam mumbled something under his breath about how that might actually be God's plan and gestured for the men to enter.

"Gentlemen," Balaam began, "I don't think that there's anything I—"

Balaam's wandering eye quickly brought a screeching halt to his line of thought when he saw a case that one of the men was opening to reveal a small, but definitely remarkable amount of treasure.

Balaam cleared his throat. "As I was saying, it's getting late, and I think it might be best if I meditate upon these things and ask the LORD what he'd have me to do."

That night the angel of the LORD appeared and with a swift kick knocked the sleeping prophet off his bed and onto the floor.

"Fasting and praying all night, are we Balaam?"

Balaam fell to his face as the LORD continued speaking. "So who's that I hear in the other room?"

Balaam trembled as he answered. "Those men are emissaries of the king of Moab, Balak; and they, um, they want to know if I can curse the children of Israel so that they can defeat them in battle."

The LORD let out a laugh so hard that it would have awakened everyone in the house, except that he only intended for Balaam to hear it.

"What makes you think I would want that? Balaam, if I were the type to be surprised about anything, I would be surprised that you would even let these people into your house! Why, you shouldn't have to ask me on something like this!"

"Well, LORD, I just wanted to make sure, and you said that men ought always to pray," Balaam sniveled.

"All right then, I'm going to give you a three point outline on this one and I expect you to pass on the message. You understand?"

"Yes, LORD."

"Now you had better mean it, for your own sake. I gave Moses a three point message and he dropped the ball. He was supposed to tell Pharaoh three things. Number one: Israel is my son. Number two: let my son go that he may serve me. And number three: if you don't let my son go I'll in turn kill your firstborn son. You remember that? He left out two-thirds of the message and found himself in a tight spot because of it.

"You don't like tight spots, do you, Balaam?"

"No, LORD."

"Okay then. This is your three point message. Number one: you cannot go with them. Number two: you can't curse Israel. Number three: Israel is already blessed of God."

"Yes, LORD, I'll deliver the message."

"Goodnight, Balaam!" the LORD said as he disappeared.

The next day over breakfast with the gentlemen
from the south, the prophet found that he just didn't
have the heart to deliver the goods. His well-polished
habit of making sure not to say anything that might
offend someone in the congregation had simply
gotten the best of him. He once again failed to deliver
the entire message entrusted to him.

"I can't go with you," he said, almost reluctantly.

"Is that what the LORD said? He said you can't
go with us? Just to see the king and talk about it?"

"That's right. You need to return into your own
country and leave me alone. That's all there is to it,
gentlemen. Good luck."

A week later, a much larger procession of
dignitaries woke Balaam up this time. They brought
all kinds of silver and gold with them, with the
promise of even greater riches, rank and honor within
the king's house. With such an opportunity for
ministry expansion, Balaam purposed in his heart to
ignore his original instructions and ask God once
more.

Never forgetting the role of pious minister,
Balaam decreed, with one hand up and his eyes
closed, that he would simply have to ask the LORD

again; and this time whatever God said would be the final answer.

That night God kicked him out of his bed again. "You know, you sleep more than any preacher I know."

"Sorry, LORD."

"I see they're back."

"Yes, LORD, may I go with them?"

"You sound awfully anxious there, Balaam. Tell you what, if they call unto you again in the morning to come and go with them, then go ahead; but make sure you only say what I tell you to say."

"Yes, LORD. Thank-you LORD."

Balaam went to sleep happy that night, but he had no idea what kind of mess into which he was putting himself. God had granted his persistent request, but had sent leanness unto his soul. In spite of this, God had given him one more chance to avoid the trouble for which he was headed.

But Balaam missed it. Instead of waiting in his room to see if the men would call on him or not, he was the first one up in the morning getting his gear packed onto his donkey. And later while riding along, Balaam considered how fortunate he was.

After all, a preacher doesn't always see an opportunity like this every day.

The preacher also didn't see the fuming angel of the LORD that was ready to lop his head off with an unsheathed broadsword. Balaam was right, however, to consider how fortunate he was because although he was blind to what was going on, his donkey wasn't. Much to Balaam's aggravation she saw the angel and veered off the path into a field. He beat her with his staff until she went back on the trail, this time behind the angel.

As to be expected the angel of the LORD took up another position on the path and stood ready to end the preacher's life as soon as he came within range. The donkey was looking out for him again and thrust herself against the wall to avoid the angel, crushing Balaam's foot in the process. He screamed in pain and anger, once again hitting the circumspect animal.

The third time the poor donkey saw the angel, there was nowhere for her to go. He had blocked the path completely and to go any further would have meant certain death for Balaam. So she laid down on the ground and Balaam lost his temper once again and let her have it with his staff.

"Why do you keep hitting me?" the donkey said.

Now normally if an animal were to speak to a man, the man wouldn't bother to actually answer the question that was being asked him. In fact, he would be more likely to pass out or run away in shock, but apparently Balaam was too concerned with arguing with a donkey to really process the fact that he was actually arguing with a donkey.

"Because you keep making me look like a neddy in front of these people. That's why I keep hitting you!"

"Pardon me; a what?" the donkey said.

"Oh never mind! Why are you even talking to me? If I had a sword I'd kill you right now! I have you to carry me and my belongings wherever I want to go, not to engage in personal debate!"

Now the donkey, being much more sensible and rational at this particular moment, spoke softly. "I am your donkey, and I've been your donkey for a very long time. Have I ever acted like this before?"

Balaam scratched his head. "Do you mean, have you ever talked to me before, or have you ever ridden off where you weren't supposed to?"

"Let's go with both, for the sake of argument," she replied.

"Um, then the answer would be no."

"Do you see that shadow on the ground, Master?" she said. "Look behind you."

Balaam's eyes had now been opened, and he saw standing behind him the angel of the LORD with a broadsword lifted up over his head, poised to strike.

"No!" Balaam screamed and fell to his face before the LORD.

The angel spoke. "You had better feed that animal of yours really well tonight, because she saved your skin three times today. Surely I would have slain thee and saved her alive."

"I have sinned, LORD! I didn't know you were angry! I had no idea that you stood against me. If what I'm doing displeases you, I'll head home right now!"

"No, you need to finish what you've started here," the LORD explained. "But I want you to only speak the words that I give you; you understand?"

"Yes, LORD," Balaam said as he stood up and dusted himself off.

The LORD placed the tip of the sword on the prophet's throat. "I believe you this time. In fact, I'm going to see to it that not only do you preach everything I tell you to, but you're going to be preaching some of the best messages anyone will ever read. In a way you're going to be famous, Balaam. How this ends is up to you; but I will have my glory, and my word will not return unto me void."

When Balaam finally reached the king, he was peppered with question after question. Balak wasn't angry; he was simply flabbergasted because with everything he had to offer Balaam hadn't come to him when he had called him.

Balaam for once had the right answer. "Well, I'm here now, your Majesty. I don't have the power to say anything of myself. Whatever God puts in my mouth, that's what I'll have to say."

The next day Balaam and the king, as well as his royal entourage, went up to the high places of the false god Baal. From that mountain vantage point the prophet was able to see all the host of Israel. Balaam ordered sacrifices to be offered on seven altars and then he went off to the side.

"All right LORD," Balaam prayed, "I'm here now and I'm ready to say whatever you want me to say."

God spoke to his heart. *Just like the good old days, Balaam?*

"Yes LORD, I'm ready."

Balaam turned and faced the king and his people, and with his right hand raised he began to prophesy. "Balak took me up to curse Jacob and to defy Israel. But how may I curse whom God hath not cursed and how shall I defy whom the LORD hath not defied?

"For from the top of the rocks I see him and from the hills I behold him: lo, the people shall dwell alone, and shall not be reckoned among the nations.

"Who can count the dust of Jacob, and the number of the fourth part of Israel? Let me die the death of the righteous, and let my last end be as that of Israel!"

The men stood dumbfounded. "What was that?" Balak said. "What did you just do to me? I asked you to curse them, not to bless them!"

"Sorry king," Balaam said. "But I'm just here to say what God wants me to say."

"Okay, okay, well, that's what I have you here for, I think," Balak replied, "But maybe if we go to another mountain you can try again?"

"I'm offering no guarantees, I'm just the messenger," Balaam said as he turned to descend the mountain.

Later atop Mount Pisgah's lofty heights Balaam raised his hand again to speak the word of God.

"Thus saith the LORD! God is not a man, that he should lie; neither the son of man, that he should repent. Hath he not spoken it? Shall he not make it good?

"He hath not seen iniquity in Jacob, neither hath he beheld perverseness in Israel: the LORD his God is with him and the shout of a king is among them!

"God himself hath brought him out of Egypt, and there is no divination against him that shall stand. It shall be said of Israel: what hath God wrought!"

"Wow," Balak said, "that was the biggest load of rubbish I've ever heard. Is this why I've called you over here, to babble on like a maniac? What do you mean there's no iniquity in Jacob? Haven't you been paying attention to how many of those people God has already killed because of their sin? Remember the fiery serpents?"

"King," Balaam said. "I'm not here to explain God's ways; I'm here to deliver his message. But if you haven't figured it out already, I'll break it down real simple for you: those people are not ordinary people. Individually God will kill anyone of them for being wicked, but as a group they're very special to him. As a nation they have the righteousness of the LORD."

"Oh never mind all that mess," Balack said, growing ever frustrated. "I've just about had it with you! I'll give you one more chance to curse them."

"Suit yourself."

And off they went to another mountain, this time it was Mount Peor. After offering sacrifices again, Balaam brought another message.

"How goodly are thy tents, O Jacob, and thy tabernacles, O Israel. As a valley are they spread forth, as gardens by the river's side. He shall pour the water out of his buckets; and his seed shall be in many waters, and his king shall be higher than Agag, and his kingdom shall be exalted.

"He brought him forth from Egypt; he hath as it were the strength of an unicorn. He shall eat up the nations, his enemies, and shall break their bones and pierce them through with arrows.

"He crouched, he lay down as a lion, and as a great lion: who shall stir him up? Blessed is he that blesseth thee, and cursed is he that curseth thee!"

Balak was irate. "What in the world are you doing? Stop blessing them! And besides all that, none of what you say is actually making any sense! One minute you sound like you're talking about a group, the next you sound like your talking about a lone man—"

Balaam interrupted. "That's called double application, your Majesty."

"I don't care about your prophecy, Balaam; I want these people gone or dead!" Balak screamed. "Now, you haven't been any help at all to me. Leave at once; go back to where you came from! You're nothing but trouble!"

"Wait, I have one final message from the LORD," Balaam said. "I think it has to do with what this people will do to thy people in the last days. Do you want to hear it?"

"Sure, why not. It's not like you can mess things up anymore than you've already done. Besides, I'm curious about the future of my people."

Balaam raised his hand again and began to speak. His eyes glossed over and lost focus as he went into a trance.

"I shall see him, but not now. I shall behold him, but not nigh. Behold, there shall come a star out of Jacob, and a scepter shall rise out of Israel, and it shall smite the corners of Moab!"

"No!" Balak screamed. "Why is this happening!?"

Balaam went right on speaking. "Israel shall do valiantly; Edom and Sier shall be a possession. Out of Jacob shall come he that shall have dominion, and shall destroy him that remained of the city. Amalek shall perish forever, the Kenite shall be wasted, alas, who shall live when God doeth this!"

"Don't you have anything good to say?" Balak said frustrated. "You're the most negative preacher I've ever heard."

"Sorry King, I'm just saying what God told me to."

"Well, did God tell you to go back where you came from, you worthless and penniless hermit? Go back to your broken-down shack up there in Pethor and die alone. You could have been rich; you could have had whatever your heart desired. Now go back home to your insignificant little life as a man of God that no one has any respect for or time to listen to. You had your chance to be rich and make a difference, and you blew it old man. You blew it."

The king's tirade cut deep, and Balaam gave place to the Devil. As Balak began to walk away, Balaam allowed the words to sink in deeper and deeper. Angels stood by the prophet, ready to drag the demons away that were tormenting him, if only he would simply ask for deliverance. He did not. Doubt turned to discouragement, and discouragement to self-pity, and self-pity led to rebellion.

"Um, King, before you go, I do have something you might be interested in hearing."

Balak turned around. "Balaam, give me one reason not to kill you where you stand."

"I can't curse them," Balaam said. "But I know how you can turn God against them. You won't have to kill them; God will kill them for you."

"How's that?" Balak responded.

"If you can't beat them," Balaam smiled, "then get them to join you."

And Israel abode in Shittim and the people began to commit whoredom with the daughters of Moab. And they called the people unto the sacrifices of the gods: and the people did eat and bowed down to their gods.

And Israel joined himself unto Baal-peor: and the anger of the LORD was kindled against Israel. Behold, these caused the children of Israel, through the counsel of Balaam, to commit trespass against the LORD in the matter of Peor, and there was a plague among the congregation of the LORD.

Chapter Twenty-One

"A good name *is* better than precious ointment; and
the day of death than the day of one's birth."
Ecclesiasties 7:1

Not Many Days Later: Shittim

Thousands were dying from the plagues that had struck the camp. The corpses were piling up faster than they could be buried. Fever, vomiting, yellow and reddish skin discolorations were the order of the day. As usual, some were calling for Moses to be stoned, others were begging for another brass serpent to be raised, but nobody really knew what to do.

It all started when the Midianites and the Moabites sent emissaries of peace, followed quickly thereafter by gifts of gold and jewels, food and wine, women and revelry. It was too hard to resist for the majority of the people, for there was something for everyone to enjoy.

And my how things had spun so quickly out of control. They had once again decided to replace the

God of their forefathers with another and in turn he had cursed them.

Balak was beside himself with joy; Balaam was well paid for his advice.

The message that Moses was receiving from God was plain: *the wages of sin is death.* God wasn't saying anything else and Moses' prayers weren't making a dent. The only conclusion that Moses could come to was that before he would turn from his wrath God wanted blood.

"Start taking the heads of the dead," Moses said to the judges of Israel, "and hang them up in the sight of God and all the people."

"Moses, that's disgusting, are you sure?"

"Sin and the consequences of sin are disgusting," Moses replied. "We have to do something to stop this plague or our children will have no chance against whatever is on the other side of Jordan because there won't be any of them left to fight.

"Men, take all of you your swords and go into the camp and slay everyone who has joined himself unto Baal."

As Moses was speaking to the men he saw off in the distance, but not too far away, a young man. His name was Zimri and he had parents who were of great influence within the house of Simeon. At this particular moment, when Moses and everyone else were watching him, he had a Midianitish woman with him. Not just any Midianitsh woman, her name was Cozbi and she was a daughter of Zur who was a high ranking member of the house of Midian. The two were laughing, flirting and generally enjoying each other's company as they headed to his tent. Moses was amazed at the audacity of the couple. Lying on the ground all around them were the corpses of people who had died from the unholy merger of their peoples. They had no sympathy for the women and children they passed who sat in the dirt weeping for their dead and dying. They showed no respect for the authority of Moses and the judges as they smiled and waived.

The tent door flap closed behind them.

Moses was about to order a command when he saw another man running towards the tent. This man was a priest who had been ministering to the sick and to those who had lost loved ones. He did not hear Moses' command given to the judges to kill the fornicators, he simply took it upon himself to grab a javelin and charge the tent. His name was Phinehas, Aaron's grandson, and when he exited the tent the happy couple was pinned to the ground, stabbed together through the stomach in a bloody mess.

After twenty–four thousand people died, God's wrath was abated because one man had enough and took action.

The months that followed were a time of spiritual healing for the people. They returned to the God of their fathers and their hearts were knit together in repentance. They mourned their losses and buried their dead.

Over the course of this time Moses gave a command to number the people. The last time he had done this they were on the cusp of crossing the Jordan River and entering into the Promised Land. A spy from every tribe searched the land and only two of them came back trusting God and optimistic about what was before them.

The other ten and the rest of the people with them were not only terrified of taking on the giants in the land, but they were getting ready to stone Joshua and Caleb for simply taking God at his word. The entire nation was complaining and murmuring about the whole situation. God and Moses were frustrated with the people, and God was ready to kill them. Moses saved their lives, once again, but it meant spending forty years wandering around in the wilderness until everyone that was twenty years and older, except for Joshua and Caleb, had died. They never saw the Promised Land, but their children were going to.

Their children, minus twenty-four thousand of them that is.

"Vex the Midianites," the LORD had said to Moses, *"and smite them: for they vexed you with their wiles."*

And now Moses stood before the people to address them. "The LORD hath said, 'Vex the Midianites,' and so we shall. Arm yourselves for war, ye men of Israel. The LORD God Jehovah shall avenge himself of Midian.

"Take heed: we are not commanded this day to send an ambassador of peace to our enemies, or to seek a place of agreement of some kind - we are commanded to bring the sword. We are not told to love our enemies, or to do good unto them, we have been given the command to destroy them and so we shall.

"The LORD hath said that all males and also all women who have known man, must be slain. A thousand soldiers of every tribe will attack the host of Midian."

The next day twelve thousand screaming Jews poured into the plains of Moab by the Jordan River. This was a whole other breed of Israelite; these young men had been raised in the desert. They had pillowed their heads on rocks at night and chased scorpions and lizards all their lives. They knew nothing of the luxuries of Egypt. They were bred warriors, perfect soldiers, having suffered persecution and endured hardness for as far back as they could remember, and they were ready for this day.

The men of Israel were faster than the Midianites. Their reaction time was more attune; they were more nimble with their feet and deft with their weapons. An enemy would lunge with the spear in vain, piercing nothing but thin air, only to lose his arm in the process having left it vulnerably outstretched. Some were too slow to recover after they had their sword deflected and were brought down by a return slash to their vitals.

The host moved through the camp like a flood, tossing torches and killing the men. For the most part, that is. There were those that attempted to break the command of the LORD and spare some, but Moses quickly put an end to that.

The old turncoat, Balaam, was found later that day. He had been killed in the street, running for his life. He had exchanged his prophet's robe for a Baalite priest's black robe of death. He had received the reward of his iniquity.

The camp of Israel was rejoicing. They had conquered the enemy and they were once again poised to enter the Promised Land. This time there was no doubting God and the shout of the king was once again with them.

Only Moses, the man who was willing to give himself over and over again to save them, would not be going with them. Having smitten the rock in disobedience the second time, God told him he would not allow him to cross the Jordan River.

Now he stood before the camp of Israel for the last time. His back was straight, his gaze was piercing and his voice was as strong as ever. He held the rod of God in his hand as he began to speak.

"The LORD came from Sinai and rose up from Seir unto them; he shined forth from Mount Paran, and he came with ten thousands of his saints. From his right hand came a fiery law unto them.

"Yea, he loved the people; all his saints are in thy hand. They sat down at thy feet, every one shall receive of thy words"

He continued speaking, blessing each and every tribe with a message from the LORD. Reuben shall be plenteous, and Judah will bring help to his people. Levi, with the Thummim and Urim, and as the keepers of the law of God, shall guide the nation spiritually. God will protect Benjamin, and the children of Joseph shall be glorious. Zebulun and Issachar shall rejoice in their goings out and in their tents.

As he spoke, the spirit of the LORD came across the people, and they were encouraged and blessed. Tears were shed at the thought that this was the last time they would see Moses. He spoke of the times that the LORD had protected them, fought for them and provided for them.

"There is none like the God of Jeshuron, who rideth upon the heaven in thy help, and on the sky in his excellency! The eternal God is thy refuge, and he shall thrust out the enemy from before thee and shall destroy them."

Then he turned to the fathers and elders of Israel. He reiterated that God had promised them the land of

Canaan and that in their generation they were going to obtain every bit of it. He told them that from the Great Sea to the river Jordan and from Kadesh-barnea all the way up to the entrance of Hamath was theirs for the taking.

In the back of their minds, the fathers understood that this promise was very different from the three-hundred thousand mile land grant that was promised to Abraham, and while the land Moses spoke of would be given to them now, there was no timetable given to Abraham's promise.

Lastly, he addressed the congregation again, giving them his final words of encouragement. He charged them with the command to take from the enemy the land that God had given them.

"Happy *art* thou, O Israel! Who *is* like unto thee, O people saved by the LORD, the shield of thy help, and who *is* the sword of thy excellency! Thine enemies shall be found liars unto thee; and thou shalt tread upon their high places."

Moses then departed and climbed yet another mountain, Mount Nebo. On the mountain, he knew he would lie down and die. His mind retraced what it could of the one hundred twenty years of his life. From a prince to a fugitive, from a recluse to a prophet, from a deliverer to a leader whose love for a people grew so strong that he would give his soul for them. History was about to witness the death of the greatest human leader of all time.

Atop Mount Nebo, a conversation took place between the God of eternity and Moses. Moses understood he wasn't to enter the Promised Land because of his sin at the waters of Meribah-Kadesh, but he accepted his fate with dignity. Jehovah took the form of the angel of the LORD and stood beside his friend. Placing his arm over Moses' shoulder he showed to him all the land of Canaan that the people would receive.

The last bit of conversation that God and Moses had was by far the most mysterious. The LORD, being the God of eternity, saw the beginning of time from the end and knew what would follow that day's events. He shared some of it with Moses.

And then he asked Moses a question.

Chapter Twenty-Two

"Yet Michael the archangel, when contending with
the devil he disputed about the body of Moses,
durst not bring against him a railing accusation, but
said, The Lord rebuke thee."
Jude 1:9

Three Days Later: Somewhere in the Land of Moab

A bluish-green haze hung in the air as the half moon illuminated the night sky. From a distance the silhouette of a man could be seen as he dug a hole in the ground. As unusual and ghoulish a sight as it already was, one might find it even stranger to notice that this man was at least seven foot tall and broadly but perfectly proportioned. Seeing a man of this stature would be certainly unusual in of itself but considering what he was wearing while he was doing what he was doing would at least be equally strange. He was dressed in a white robe with gold trimmings, and he had a sword on him. Not just any sword mind you, it was a broadsword with a blade of some kind of material that glowed white. The cross guard and hilt was of pure gold marked with the seal of Jehovah God. To intensify the oddity of the whole ordeal, what, or rather who, the man was digging up might be called into question.

Michael the archangel had taken a physical form in order to interact with dirt and shovel to dig up the body of Moses. It was about three days after God had personally buried him somewhere in a valley within the land of Moab. Moses was one hundred and twenty years old when he died upon Mt. Nebo, but you would have never guessed it. He wasn't sick when he died, he hadn't lost his hearing, and his eyesight was just as good as ever; in other words he hadn't died of any natural causes. He just died, because God was done using him. Or so it seemed.

From various directions five shadows crawled and crept towards the angel who was hard at work. The shadows absorbed any light around them, as if they were a vacuum of blackness. The sound of their movement hissed and popped as they slid forward.

One sprung, like a lion from the tall grass, towards the archangel. Michael slapped it down with the blade of his shovel and placed his foot on the back of the demon, effectively pinning it to the ground. While he pulled his sword from its scabbard he muttered something about the tediousness of having to deal with this and be a grave robber at the same time. The next moment there was a flash of light, a quick and almost surgical slash, a scream and two membranous horned wings fell to the ground and turned to ash. Michael then flung the monster skyward, up through the atmosphere and beyond.

He smiled at the other four that were approaching him. "You won't be seeing him for awhile."

The beasts snarled and reared back, flashing their talons and fangs. They pounced upon him in quick succession. The first one lost its two front legs and rolled to the side. Michael deflected the second, sending it tumbling with a well-placed backhand. Grabbing the third one in the middle of its attack, he threw it against a giant boulder, stunning it for a spit second. The archangel then harpooned it in place with his sword. The fourth demon latched onto Michael's back, clawing, scratching and biting. He grasped at it, desperately trying to get a hold on it and pull it off of him. Successfully apprehending a loose limb, Michael pulled the vicious thing off and slammed it to the ground repeatedly like a rag. Then he threw it skyward, just like before.

It retained its wings and after recovering it unfurled them and banked around to dive towards the Prince of Israel. Not having his sword any longer Michael was entangled in a wrestling match with the demon he had just backhanded, which by now had recovered. He cast it against the boulder next to the skewered beast that was screaming for someone to free it.

As the flying demon closed in, Michael ran towards the boulder. The thing was nearly on top of him by now, rapidly closing in behind him. In an instant when it appeared Michael would be struck down, he finally reached his sword. In one smooth motion he pulled his sword out and pointed the tip of the blade towards the flyer, which shrieked as it stabbed itself upon it. Michael then grabbed the other three fallen angels and stuck them on the blade, like an olive on a toothpick. Flying high in the air, he threw the sword to where it fastened in the middle of the Euphrates River, trapping the four fallen angels underwater.

Returning back to the burial site, he saw he had another visitor.

"Nicely done, but that's the ugliest shish-kabob I've ever seen," Satan said with a smile. "I never thought you could pin four on a sword. That has to be a new record for you."

Michael wasn't amused and went back to digging.

The Devil wouldn't leave him alone. "You know, you're going to need a new sword now."

Michael grunted a response as he tossed another shovelful of dirt to the side.

"Mike," Satan said as he placed a hand on his shoulder, "you don't mind if I call you Mike, do you?"

Michael knocked Satan's hand off his shoulder and went back to digging.

Satan took a step back. "Okay, we'll stick with Michael. Why so hostile, Michael? Are you against have a friendly conversation?"

Michael looked up and exhaled, "Satan–"

"Call me Lucifer," Satan interrupted.

"You don't deserve that name anymore."

"But it's still my name."

"It doesn't mean what it used to."

"I like changing things up a little, don't you?"

Michael paused and just looked at him. "The LORD rebuke you, Satan. I'm not interested in arguing with you or fighting you."

"Good thing," Satan said baiting him. "I don't think you'd do all that well against me with that shovel."

"The LORD rebuke you."

"Why is that your go-to move, Mike? Don't you have anything better than that?"

Michael eyes flashed with anger but his tone was measured, "Not by my might, nor by my power, but by his spirit. I don't have any strength over you. I don't have any strength at all outside of God's power. I have no problem understanding and admitting that. That's the difference between the Lucifer I knew, and the Satan you are today."

Satan took another step back. "Okay, okay, I'm sorry I was so forward. So what are you doing digging up Moses' body for anyway?"

"God wants it."

Satan laughed. "Of course he does, but why?"

"Don't you have better things to do?"

"Actually, Michael, I don't. I had plans for that body. I think it would make an excellent idol."

Michael pulled the casket out of the hole and up to the surface.

Satan went on. "You know, technically, God really doesn't have any right to this body. In a round about way, I get to corrupt everyone's bodies because they all have sin on them. I see to it everyone rots. God's actually breaking a rule here–"

"Just like he did with Enoch?" Michael interrupted. He put Moses' body over his shoulder.

"Before you go," Satan said. "Would you mind telling me at least why God is taking the body? Unless, of course, he specifically told you not to say anything. Could you tell me please, you know, for old time's sake, Michael?"

Michael looked at him and in that brief moment of time the Deceiver actually managed to strike a chord with the archangel. Michael's mind flashed back to the joy of creation day as he and Gabriel, along with Lucifer, shouted and sang the praises of Jehovah as loud as angelically possible. The visage of the chief musician that day was nothing like what stood before him now and in a moment of weakness Michael felt sympathy for his former friend.

"The reason Moses' body never became feeble is the same reason I'm taking it now: he's going to need it again just the way it is."

"Thanks buddy!" Satan said in mocking laughter as he vanished into thin air, and Michael realized he'd been had.

Chapter Twenty-Three

"The LORD recompense thy work, and a full reward be given thee of the LORD God of Israel, under whose wings thou art come to trust."
Ruth 2:12

1422 B.C.: Shittim

"Moses my servant is dead."

The words rattled Joshua to the bone as the LORD spoke them. God was telling him to fill the shoes of his hero. Joshua, as a nineteen year old, was a slave leaving the brick foundries of Egypt and had been Moses' right hand man ever since he was twenty-one. Now he was sixty, and he was being asked to pick up where Moses had left off.

"Now therefore arise, go over this Jordan, thou, and all this people, unto the land which I do give to them. Every place that the sole of your foot shall tread upon, that have I given to you, as I said unto Moses."

Joshua knew the cost. He had spent the last forty years fighting. He fought heat exhaustion and sandstorms, Amelikites and Midianites and scorpions and rattlesnakes.

He knew that he was just getting started.

Like any experienced soldier, Joshua had had a moment of fear that he wasn't particularly proud of but he kept it to himself. It may have been on Mount Sinai, when he had accompanied Moses to receive the law. The thunders, lightings, flashes of fire, and the booming voice of the LORD would be enough to terrify any man. It may have been his first military engagement or perhaps the roar of Pharaoh's chariots behind him as he crossed the Red Sea. Whenever it was and whatever it was, that same fear had once again wrapped its deadly tentacles around Joshua's heart today as God addressed him.

The LORD knew this and encouraged his servant. "There shall not any man be able to stand before thee all the days of thy life: as I was with Moses, so I will be with thee. I will not fail thee, nor forsake thee."

There it was again, the reference to Moses. Those were big shoes to fill and certainly any man who found himself in Joshua's position would wrestle with self-doubt. God was asking him to take the place of the man who had delivered Israel from

Egypt, wrought signs and wonders among the people, and parted the Red Sea.

It should be no problem.

The LORD read his mind. "Joshua, Moses didn't do any of those things on his own. I did them. I'm going to be with you as I was with him. Do not be afraid, only trust the LORD with all thine heart and lean not unto thine own understanding. I used Moses to show my people the law and deliver them from bondage; you are going to make them conquerors and give them the abundant life that comes with my promises."

Joshua's heart was encouraged, but the thought of spending the rest of his life fighting was still daunting.

God interrupted his thoughts again. "Only be strong, Joshua, and of a good courage. I will give this land unto the people, and you will be the one to divide it out to them. You will find rest in Canaan."

Joshua was certainly up to the challenge and was encouraged to know that unlike Moses he would be there once the land had been conquered. His next concern was quite naturally how long he would have to fight before he received that coveted rest.

"Joshua," the LORD said, "I didn't choose you because of your ability to give a speech or motivate men. I'm not interested in a politician or an educator. I'm not even looking for a prophet or a preacher. I want a soldier with a loyal heart. I'll take one loyal soldier that keeps his mouth shut and does his duty over a hundred eloquent prophets with divided loyalties like Balaam. I want you because you're a soldier, Joshua; I want you because I know I can trust you to follow an order.

"Yes, you will spend the majority of the rest of your life fighting. There will be constant battle with the enemy in this life, there's no escaping it long term. You can either give in to the enemy and go into bondage, or give in to me and battle for liberty – there is no neutral ground.

"Being a good fighter and military commander in the battles to come will not be enough. You need me. Only be thou strong and very courageous, that thou mayest observe to do all according to the law which Moses my servant commanded thee: turn not from it to the right hand or to the left."

Joshua's heart was once again strengthened, but the fleeting thought of fighting a nine foot tall son of Anak gave him another cause for concern.

In his everlasting patience, love and kindness, the LORD who is a Man of War addressed that concern as well. "Joshua, don't you remember my friend Abraham? He already fought these giants once before. Don't you remember that he did it with a rag-tag army of only three hundred men? They weren't exactly hardened soldiers as you have here. They were much better at cooking and herding sheep than swinging a sword, and yet I was with them and they defeated the armies of four different nations. Now if I can do that with them, what do you think I can do with you?

"What I'm getting at is that the challenge you face isn't new. Other men have done things like this before with far fewer resources than you have at your disposal. I will be with you, Joshua! I'll never put something in front of you that you can't handle.

"Should the day come that you're having trouble trusting me and it seems that what I've done for you isn't enough, then look at what I've done for others. You must steel your mind for the challenge that lies before you, for that is where the real battle takes place.

"Have not I commanded thee? Be strong and of a good courage; be not afraid, neither be thou dismayed: for the LORD thy God is with thee whithersoever thou goest!"

And so Joshua's commission was not all that different from Moses'. Moses had wrestled with fear and doubt and while he was much more vocal about it than Joshua, he too raised objections as to what God was asking of him. The LORD patiently answered all objections and fears and brought both men to where he needed them. Both believed themselves not to be ready; they felt stretched, inadequate for the job and that the task was too great.

Yet, once they looked away from the problems to come and toward the God of their fathers, their hearts told them that nothing is impossible with God.

Chapter Twenty-Four

"What *ailed* thee, O thou sea, that thou fleddest?
thou Jordan, *that* thou wast driven back?"

Psalm 114:5

Six Days Later: The Banks of the Jordan River

The words of the people reverberated in Joshua's mind. *We will hearken unto thy commandment: only the LORD thy God be with thee, as he was with Moses.*

Joshua stood looking at the Jordan River as he pondered that thought. Now indeed would be a good time for the LORD to be with him as he was with Moses.

After leaving Shittim and arriving at Jordan, the last three days were a time of wait-and-see in the Israelite camp. Finally the spies had returned and brought the good news: the hearts of the Canaanites had melted at the thought of the Jewish invasion force right outside their door. The only thing stopping them, or rather slowing them down, was the natural defensive border provided by the Jordan River.

"It's nice that there's no army chasing us this time," Caleb mentioned to Joshua as he walked by to join up with the other eleven men hand-picked for a special task. Meanwhile, two wooden staves overlaid with gold supported the Ark of the Covenant as it was lifted up and carried towards the river by the Levitical priests.

Moments ago Joshua had just finished promising everyone another miracle. As he watched the priests, Joshua registered Caleb's comment, agreeing that truer words could not be spoken. This was in fact a different miracle for a different time and for a different group of people. When Moses parted the sea, the expectations were pretty low. Nobody was expecting it, if anything they were all just expecting to be wiped out, but then the LORD came out of the middle of nowhere to save the day.

This time there was no sense of urgency, and if things didn't work out, no one was going to die. In fact, the people could still cross the river; it was just going to be a hassle. A really big hassle considering the water was moving pretty fast, the river was about forty-five feet wide, and the depth was well over a man's head.

But besides those difficulties, something else was at stake: the confidence of the people in Joshua's leadership. This was the first test. If things didn't work out as he said they would, then trusting Joshua later when lives would indeed be on the line, would be much more difficult.

And so the priests walked and the people watched. As soon as their feet touched the water, the same mighty rushing wind came again. This time instead of parting a body of unmoving water, the water that flowed from the north stalled. The men placed their feet on dry ground and as they walked the water to their left kept flowing, without any water to replace it. To their right, all the water that was supposed to flow south, from the Sea of Chinneroth, was piling up. The people stood in awe as they saw the wall of water grow and swell, moving, churning and glistening in the midday sun.

196

The children squealed in glee and scurried across the river bed. They ran their fingers through the throbbing wall of water as they hopped and skipped their way to the other side. Their parents laughed as they followed behind.

As soon as all the people were clean passed over, other than the priests who had stopped halfway through, Joshua sent the twelve men back. Each one of them found a heavy stone and placed it on their shoulder, carrying it back to the river bank. Bearing the Ark of the Covenant, the priests left the dry ground of the river bed, and as soon as their feet touched the dry ground of the river bank, the water gently slid back into place.

That evening the people camped at Gilgal. They rejoiced again in the mighty hand of God as they laughed and told stories around campfires late into the night. The stones were placed in a heap, one from every tribe, as a memorial to what God had done for them that day. The people had full confidence in Joshua, and Joshua had full confidence in the LORD as he addressed the congregation.

"When your children shall ask their fathers in time to come, saying, 'What mean these stones?' Then ye shall let your children know, saying, Israel came over this Jordan on dry land. For the LORD your God dried up the waters of Jordan from before you, until ye were passed over, as the LORD your God did to the Red Sea, which he dried up from before us, until we were gone over: that all the people of the earth might know the hand of the LORD, that it is mighty: that ye might fear the LORD your God for ever."

Chapter Twenty-Five

"The LORD *is* a man of war: the LORD *is* his name."
Exodus 15:3

Six Days Later: Jericho

The morale of the people could not be higher. They were right with God, they were blessed of God and ready for a fight. Having struggled and fought their way to the doorstep of Canaan, they were eager to take that which God had already given to them hundreds of years ago.

Like a cup that overflowed, Joshua was full of courage as well. Ready to tackle whichever task that lie before him and fight whatever enemy stood in his way, he wasn't going to be intimidated by anything.

In spite of the spirit of the people, they had hit a roadblock: Jericho. Considered to be the oldest city in existence, it was also very well protected by six foot thick stone walls. Joshua was perplexed as to what to do. No one was coming out, and it looked as if no one was going in either.

His best solution at this time was to simply starve the people out into an attack. Food was certainly available for the Israelites; in fact once they had starting eating the food of Canaan, they noticed that the manna had stopped coming down.

Although some were milling about that morning, most of the camp was still asleep. Joshua pondered his current military situation alone as he watched the sunrise in the distance paint the sky.

Something distracted the commander for a moment; looking back he saw the silhouette of a massive soldier with his sword drawn heading straight for him.

It's one of those cursed Anakims, Joshua thought to himself. Sliding his sword out of its sheath he rose to meet the figure that approached him.

Standing in front of him, Joshua had never before seen a soldier of this kind. He stood head and shoulders over Joshua. The armor he wore was not of this world. Though solid in form, it seemed to move, shimmering and refracting colors as light off a droplet of water. The stranger rested his hands on the hilt of the sword, with the tip of the blade in the dirt, and stood there silently looking at Joshua.

Joshua didn't care if he was being sized up or not. He didn't care if the stranger was bigger and stronger than he. He didn't care how pretty his armor was or how tough he was. The way he saw it, he was going to be fighting giants for a long time, and now was as good a time as any to become used to the idea.

"Whose side are you on?" Joshua said as he tightened the grip on his weapon. "Ours or theirs?"

The armed man before him placed his sword away, removed his helmet and smiled. "Nay, but as captain of the host of the LORD am I now come."

Within a split second, Joshua realized that he was standing before the very person of God himself. Dropping his sword, he fell to his face and worshipped.

"What saith my lord unto his servant?"

The next words the LORD spoke were not without irony. "You're on holy ground Joshua; take off your shoes."

Once again, as he had said to Moses before him concerning Horeb, God was telling Joshua that this land was holy as well. This land that would be soaked in the blood of saints and sinners, soldiers and martyrs, was Canaan land, the holy Promised Land.

Joshua arose and quickly removed his shoes as the LORD explained the battle plan.

"Joshua, I want you to take your best soldiers, your elite soldiers, and walk around Jericho one time each day for six days without saying anything."

Not exactly a plan that Joshua envisioned, but by now he was learning to expect the unexpected.

The LORD continued. "I want the priests to carry the Ark around the city with you, in the middle of the procession. Make sure to have seven other priests walk in front of them carrying trumpets.

On the seventh day have them all go around the city seven times and then blow the horns for a long time. When they're finished, I want everyone to shout. If you do that, the walls will fall down and the city will be yours."

"I'll relay the command right away, LORD."

"One last thing, this city is the firstfruit, it's mine. Command the people to not take of the spoil for themselves; it is to go into my treasury. Understood?"

"Yes, LORD."

"Well done, Joshua," the LORD said placing his helmet back on his head. He gave his servant one last look and then disappeared in a flash of white and blue.

The mighty men of Israel followed their orders to the letter. They silently marched while out of range of the tower's boulders and held shields over their heads to protect themselves from the arrows shot at them. After the first few days, the men of Jericho went from firing at the Jews to laughing at them.

On the seventh day, the heat was suffocating and the shields were heavy, but the men kept marching. They had full assurance in Joshua and the command given by the angel of the LORD. The remainder of the people watched with anticipation. Though they were silent, they were pulling for the men of war in their hearts.

At the sound of the trump, everything broke loose. The nation of Israel, numbering well over a million strong, roared at the top of their lungs. The ground shook, enemy soldiers were knocked off of parapets, and the walls of Jericho swelled from the inside-out. In a mighty crash they broke and fell down flat.

The marching men were the shock troops. Scrambling over and between the walls, they rushed into the city like ants. The soldiers of Jericho were much fewer in number and in complete shock, wholly unprepared for the moment. Completely overwhelmed once the rest of the Israelite army had broken through, the entire population of Jericho was wiped out in a matter of minutes.

Once again, the people of God sang praises that night and rejoiced in the victory the LORD had wrought. But just as the men of Jericho were unprepared for what had hit them, so too Joshua was entirely caught off guard by what would happen next.

Chapter Twenty-Six

"There was not a word of all that Moses commanded, which Joshua read not before all the congregation of Israel, with the women, and the little ones, and the strangers that were conversant among them."

Joshua 8:35

The Next Day: Jericho

T he next stop on the military campaign was a little town by the name of Ai. Joshua had a particular interest in that city because it was close to Bethel, the place that Jacob had seen the ladder and that God had reaffirmed his covenant unto him. He wanted that ground back.

Having gone through quite an ordeal at Jericho, Joshua dispatched a small group of men to scout out Ai and to see what they were up against.

When they returned, the message was clear: Ai is small and ill-prepared to defend against an attack. There was no need to dispatch tens of thousands to defeat them; an army of about three thousand should do the job.

Mothers and children waived as the soldiers departed and hearts filled with pride at the sight of them. But off to the side, standing in the doorway of his tent, was a man by the name of Achan. He watched as the wives embraced their husbands, and little boys hugged their fathers. He wondered what was going to happen next.

If one could look past the man standing in the doorway, a pile of freshly moved dirt could be seen in the middle of his tent. Beneath the soil lay a Babylonish garment, two hundred shekels of silver and a wedge of gold. Achan had disobeyed the command not to take of the spoil of Jericho. He had taken what belonged to God, and as a result, a curse had fallen on the children of Israel. Watching the detachment fade off into the distance, Achan remembered the words of Joshua: *And ye, in any wise keep yourselves from the accursed thing, lest ye make yourselves accursed, when ye take of the accursed thing, and make the camp of Israel a curse, and trouble it.*

The men of Israel rushed upon Ai. Recoiling at the gate of the city, they fell into a bottleneck. The formation was such that for every one Jew that was trying to break through, there were two defenders there to hold them back. Just to the inside of the gate, behind shield and spear, the men of Ai held their ground.

The Jews pushed as if against a stone wall. Shield crashed against shield as those in the rear heard the frustrated shouts of the men on the front.

"Push, men, push," one groaned. "We must break through!" A spear slithered forward from the top of a shield and pierced his collarbone, bringing him down to the ground.

Pounding rain turned the ground into ankle deep sludge. A man slipped and fell upon his own sword. Beside him another lost his footing, his shield dipping just long enough for an enemy to run him through. Relentless, there was no hiatus for the darting spearheads and the faceless wall of shields was impenetrable.

At last, hope seemed to flee when all Hebrew eyes tuned to a familiar face. It was a man of valour, Jazer, battling for his God and his people. A short man, but massive, he was built like an ox; his strength and speed were rarely matched. Jazer was on the cusp of breaching the line and turning the tide. His blade tore through the men of Ai like a reaper through a wheat field.

But the world seemed to move at an awkwardly rapid pace now. Jazer roared as a spear pierced his thigh. He snapped the end off and shoved it through the belly of the offender. Falling backwards now, he just missed being run through by another. "Not like this!" he grunted, scrambling on his stomach for his sword. A boot sent it flying through the air and the hero rolled to his back to face the death blow.

"No!" Othniel screamed, slamming his shield into the torso of the man who stood poised over Jazer. His sickle-sword finished the dazed opponent quickly. "We've got to get you out of here," Othniel cried, his youthful face filled with tears and rage.

"We all must flee," Jazer winced as others came to his aid. "God isn't in this, and we're all done for if we stay any longer."

And so the men of Israel turned and fled before the men of Ai, and they pursed them from before the gate even unto Shebarim, and smote them in the going down: wherefore the hearts of the people melted and became as water.

A mournful stillness filled the camp of Israel that day. They were reminded of the fact that they were not invincible.

Near the Ark of the Covenant, Joshua and the elders of Israel lay prostrate. Their clothes were torn and they lay face first in the dust and dirt. All day without a sound they prayed.

The silence was broken at eventide. "Alas, LORD God," Joshua wept, "why did you bring us over Jordan into this land, just to die at the hands of the Amorites? I thought you said you would never leave me nor forsake me? Would to God we had just been content to dwell on the other side of Jordan!

"What shall I say when Israel turneth their backs to their enemies? They will all hear of this day and gather themselves against us and cut off our name from off the earth. And then what of thy good name?"

The LORD spoke. "Get thee up; why liest thou upon thy face?"

Quite naturally, in his mind this was not what Joshua expected to hear, but then again Joshua wasn't in the right frame of mind to begin with. Complaining to God about forward-moving obedience and daring to suggest that complacency would free him of conflict was certainly unusual for the leader of Israel. He almost sounded like some other Israelites who questioned the wisdom of leaving the leeks and garlics of Egypt.

But a day's events can change the heart of any soldier, and in this soldier's heart all the courage, bravado and faith he had lay dead and dying in a medical tent in the middle of camp. From the heights of the Jordan River crossing, to the visitation of the angel of the LORD, to the miraculous victory at Jericho, this great bastion of valor had been cut down fast and hard. He was low and despondent. None of it mattered anymore. Past victories and glories were irrelevant.

"Israel hath sinned," the LORD continued. "And they have transgressed my covenant which I commanded them: for they have taken of the accursed thing."

Listening to the LORD, Joshua was about to have something that he had given mental ascent to for decades sink from his head down to his heart. It was something that Moses had to learn as well, having seen thousands die by not taking heed to it.

"Therefore the children of Israel could not stand before their enemies, but turned their backs before their enemies, because they were accursed: neither will I be with you any more, except ye destroy the accursed from among you."

The words pierced his heart: *neither will I be with you any more, except ye destroy the accursed from among you.* The covenant was conditional. The blessings, power and guidance of the LORD were dependent upon submission and obedience. Israel needed God sorely; they were sojourners and warriors in a strange land and to lack the power of God meant annihilation.

The next day the problem was dealt with in entirety. Early in the morning, within the camp of Israel, Achan was identified as the culprit. He confessed to what he had done, and he and his family were stoned and their bodies burned. By the end of the day, the city of Ai was destroyed and the slain corpse of the king of Ai hung from a tree.

Once the whole ordeal was finished, Joshua built an altar unto the LORD in Mt. Ebal and wrote the Law of Moses down again in the sight of all Israel. He read the law to the people and made it a point to ensure that all understood it, from the little ones all the way to the strangers and elderly among them. Dozens of innocent people had died because of the actions of one man. The nation of Israel, having already discovered that with God they could part rivers and bring down mighty walls, learned that without him they would certainly fall before their enemies.

A holy fear took hold of them.

Chapter Twenty-Seven

"And there was no day like that before it or after it,
that the LORD hearkened unto the voice of a man:
for the LORD fought for Israel."
Joshua 10:14

1422 B.C.: Gibeon

The royal city of Gibeon stood defiant before the horde of Amorites encamped around it. Invisible now, but through the dark of night their lights were seen as they were heard working, cutting trees and preparing for the next day. They had come suddenly, through the forests and over the hills, an alliance forged by the king of Jerusalem, Adonizedek.

The chief elder gazed over the parapets of the city, considering the situation he found himself in. Refusing the word of the angel, he had saved his people by tricking Israel into an alliance that was against the covenant of their God. But Joshua was not his problem now.

His ponderings were quickly interrupted by garrison's commander, Bazor. "Rabanac, he made it through."

"Thank-you."

"Very well sir. Do you have any specific orders?"

"No, none," a thoughtful Rabanac said, still peering over edge. "Just occupy until he comes. If he does come."

"Yes sir."

Rabanac raised his hand, as if to signal Bazor to remain. "Fate is not without its sense of irony, isn't it?"

"What do you mean, sir?"

"Jacob lied to Esau to save his skin too."

"I'm sorry, sir. I don't follow you."

"We lied to Joshua thinking it would put us in a better place. All Joshua has to do to relieve himself from his oath is not to show up, or to show up late. We thought to protect ourselves from Israel but never considered our neighbors. Now instead of fearing the children of Israel, we need them."

"This land wherein we dwell," Bazor replied, "has no sense of neutrality. Any friend of Joshua is an enemy of everyone else."

"So it seems," Rabanac answered. "And now we'll see if Joshua is a friend to us. We may live among the Canaanites, but tomorrow will show very clearly that we are not of them. Take courage my son and play the man for the cities of Gibeon."

The few souls that managed to sleep that night were rudely interrupted by the soft beating of Canaanite war drums in the distance. The city was completely surrounded as the enemy approached it from every angle possible. There were two gates to the city, one on the north and one on the south. They would most likely bear the brunt of the attack. Having vastly outnumbered the men of Gibeon, the idea of starving them out for months on end seemed unnecessary and impractical to the enemy. A war of attrition was exactly what they wanted.

Bazor stood upon a wall facing the mighty men of Gibeon numbering in the thousands. The crisp, cold air revealed his breath as he stood before the men, ready to give a few last words before they all met their death. With a defiant smile of camaraderie, he raised open palms and began to speak.

"Oh my friends, my fellow warriors of Gibeon, Adonizedek will live to rue this day!"

They all bellowed back their support, waiving their weapons in the air.

"Apparently, to even the odds, today he's brought four other nations with him!"

More laughter and cheering were heard among the men.

"Each of you know your station and duty, and I trust all of you to perform that which is required of you. You can expect no quarter given by our enemies; our alliance with Joshua has ensured that. This battle will come down to every last man.

"I have heard it said that those who bless the armies of Israel will be blessed by the God of Israel. Today you fight against their enemies; perhaps their God will fight for you as well.

"Nevertheless, lift up the bow and sword today with honor. Ye be men of Gibeon, a mighty and royal people! And now, as ye rise to your stations, be of good courage, ye are Hivites and should ye die the death of a warrior, let it be with a cry in your heart and a sword in your fist!"

The drums beat louder and louder as the armies approached. From the north and south grotesquely huge and obese giants came in pairs, carrying trees over their shoulders, flanked by archers and spearmen. On the east and west swordsmen advanced with bands of cavalry swarming them.

Upon reaching archer range, there was no hesitation for the marching soldiers. As though possessed by an unholy disregard for their own lives, they stumbled forward. On the walls, bowstrings snapped and for a brief moment the arrows hung in the air beautifully and silently. The silence was broken as soldiers slumped to the ground by the scores.

"Keep it up men," Bazor said as he walked through the ranks. "They're not going to stop coming." Looking back over the edge he saw a pair of giants had taken the lead where others had fallen. They lumbered forward, unhindered by the arrows stuck in their legs and arms, each holding one end of a massive tree.

"Take those things down!" Bazor yelled to the men.

"We've already hit them, sir, but they won't go down!"

"Then keep hitting them!"

The arrows flew again, pinging off the giant's amour for the most part, a few here and there sticking.

"We must stop those monsters from reaching the gate," Bazor said to a company commander.

"Well, what we're doing isn't working."

"Then tell your men to ignore the giants and focus on the main group."

Bazor left the commander disconcerted, but he knew his orders. The archers kept the fire up on the main advancing body. Hundreds lay dead and dying, but the more they fired, the more they missed, and the more soldiers straggled through the hail of arrows to the front. The problem of the giants remained unsolved.

To the soldiers on the wall the level of frenzy was so high that it could have been minutes or even hours that passed. The Anakims were nearly at their wall. Both north and south gates stood vulnerable, still, almost quiet.

The giants charged forward, closing their eyes as they braced for impact. Without any warning, the gates flew open and the giants stumbled in. Four bewildered titans of power stood there silently, two on the south end of the city and two on the north. They stared for a brief moment at dozens of archers who had them in their sights at nearly point blank range.

"Welcome to Gibeon," Bazor smiled. "I hope you enjoy your stay." A few seconds later they lay dead on the ground.

The gates remained opened for a moment as several detachments of Gibeonite cavalry poured out. Row after row of giants continued to stream forward undaunted by the lethal downpour. Gibeonite archers stopped for a moment, giving the horsemen the time they needed to spread out and eliminate any stragglers.

Feeling confident, a group of four spun towards a pair of giants. In one smooth motion a Gibeonite took off the head of the first monster, but the other one ducked. He came up with his shoulder, knocking the horse to the ground. Snatching the rider off the ground, he threw him at the others, bringing them down as well. The beast was upon them and they were dead within moments.

From the wall, Bazor took a deep breath and made a motion to signal the horsemen to return. Some were already being shot at by Canaanite archers and it was clear that the enemy was reforming.

Time passed slowly as the men on the wall watched and waited, the day half spent. Clouds of dust formed as the allied armies of Adonizedek positioned themselves for another attack. Overwhelming numbers had failed in the first wave. It was clear that his commanders had underestimated Gibeon.

The ranks combined this time, with a spearman or a swordsman marching directly next to an archer. But for the tree bearing giants in the middle and the cavalry on the outskirts, one would have thought it a disorganized mess. Once again the horde was heading straight for them.

"Archers at the ready," Bazor belted out as he paced the wall. They notched their arrows and raised their bows in anticipation.

Bazor turned to the men on the ground. "Reinforce the outer and inner gates. Prepare a standard secondary line of defense at the inner wall. If they breach the outer wall, we must keep them from entering the city."

As he spoke, he heard the commanders beside him yell to their companies. He turned to see the advance was moving much faster than before and there were no reserves; they were all committed this time. *"They were just testing us before,"* he thought.

The arrows rained upon them again, but for every archer there was a man with a shield next to him. They held the shields up in defense and while the strategy was far from perfect it worked well enough.

The enemy archers returned fire. Their attacks were sloppy and inaccurate, but the absolute volume of arrows made it effective as scores of Hivites died upon every volley. All the while, they kept moving forward.

The first row of giants had almost reached the door. The rain of death on the wall was thick and getting thicker. Bazor picked up a bow from the dead soldier next to him and released an arrow that struck the first monster in the forehead. He fell backwards with a thud, smashing a couple of his countrymen.

The harder they fall, Bazor thought.

"Fall back!" Bazor shouted. There was no time for another shot for him or anyone else. There simply weren't enough archers for two walls.

"We're to abandon our posts, sir?" a zealous soldier said.

"If we stay any longer there won't be enough of us to defend the city. Now, to the inner wall immediately, we'll have to hold them there. This wall is breached."

The inner wall. As the final line of defense for the city its main tactical advantage was that it had two entrances that faced it, they were the outer gates, which served to funnel the enemy in a controlled and predictable manner.

Or at least they were supposed to; Bazor was outnumbered twenty to one. He realized he had just lost the battle of the air, where he had his greatest advantage. This brawl was about to go to the ground, and a deep sickening feeling threatened to overtake the brave man as he knew it wouldn't last long.

His thoughts went to his wife and family, huddled within the city. There would be no mercy from what was outside that door, and if they survived, it only meant facing a fate worse than death at the hands of vile and depraved men.

On the third slam the doors crashed open and enemy swordsmen flooded through the door. They were quickly cut down by archer fire, but others ran past. They were stopped and then merely slowed as the Gibeonites on the ground began falling back.

A giant surged forward, swinging a broadsword as long as a man. Bazor watched in horror as gruesome titans hacked and hurled men through the air.

He raised his bow to fire.

Bazor aimed for the behemoth of a man, the shaft of his arrow resting on his hand. He instinctively closed one eye, wanting to make this shot count, knowing he didn't have many left. About to release the string, something caused him to pause. He was completely perplexed as to what he was looking at.

The giant dropped his sword and fell to the ground. He was screaming and squirming, writhing in pain. All around him his fellow soldiers were doing the same. Some ran as though mad and blind, brushing at their heads and bodies. Bazor watched the confusion, aiming down the shaft of his notched arrow, that is until something small touched his hand which held the bow.

It was a hornet. In the midst of the screams of agony and confusion, a hornet, of all things, landed on his hand. It took a few steps, looked around and then flew towards the enemy soldiers before him.

Through the cries of men and humming of hornets, he heard a trumpet sound ringing out in the distance. It was loud and clear, coming from the hills. It was Joshua, standing to deliver the people of Gibeon. His army flowed, from east to west, onto the battlefield.

Bazor raised his hands and shouted, "The LORD God of Joshua fights for our people! He fights for us too! Praise the LORD God of Joshua!"

His men, with joy on their face, echoed his call. "All praise to the LORD God of Joshua!" They tore into the suffering Canaanites, putting them out of their misery. Within minutes not an enemy remained who entered the gates, and Bazor's men moved quickly to shore up the defenses again on the outer wall.

Outside the camp, stood Joshua. He surveyed the battlefield and saw that the enemy was turning their attention away from Gibeon and towards him. He preferred it that way. Where others saw an obstacle, he saw a golden opportunity.

We're running out of daylight, Joshua thought, *we need to finish them here.*

He watched as horses were struck with blindness; they ran in every direction, completely uncontrollable and unpredictable. The riders fell off them, writhing and convulsing on the ground, their minds filled with madness.

All the children of Israel looked to Joshua as he raised his staff in the sky. They expected him to issue an attack order of some kind, only he did something that was completely unheard of.

Filled with faith and with the permission of God Almighty, he gave nature an order. Joshua lifted his staff to the sky and cried, "Sun, stand thou still upon Gibeon; and thou, moon, in the valley of Ajalon."

Israeli swordsmen stabbed and slashed the enemy horsemen all over the field of battle. The

Canaanites were reeling and disorganized. They had no archer support, and all their cavalry lay fallen.

But they still had their giants. Fifty formed together and charged a small company of Jewish soldiers.

"Hold this ground, men," the Jewish commander said. "This day we fight and if needs be, die for our LORD and people."

The giants pounded forward; the ground shook with every step. The men of Israel fell to one knee holding their swords forward like spears, hoping against hope that they could stop their impending doom.

Time slowed as blood, sweat, and dirt hung in the air. The monstrosities backhanded whoever happened to cross their path, sending them flying. The commander drowned his terror by shouting the order again: "Hold!" Sounds of the battlefield muddled and shook in their heads: the pounding of the giant's feet, horsemen crying out in the distance, the buzzing of hornets near Gibeon. But now they heard something different; it came towards them, screaming through the sky behind them.

A massive boulder struck the lead giant in the chest and knocked him backwards like a ragdoll. The rocks came faster now, and the ground exploded as they struck it. Dirt slapped the faces of the swordsmen as they watched the wrath of God bring down the terrors of Anak. Their eyes looked upwards and across the entire field as they saw hailstones pounding the enemies of Jehovah into the ground.

Othniel and Caleb fought side by side as the world around them was exploding. The rush of battle filled their hearts as they saw the last desperate attempt by the enemy fail. The sons of Israel cut them down. Every stone and arrow hit its target. Every blade cut deeper and faster than what was humanly possible. The enemy was slowed, reckless and confused.

The tide had turned and the enemy fled in panic. The order from Joshua was clear: "Pursue after your enemies, and smite the hindmost of them; suffer them not to enter into their cities: for the LORD your God hath delivered them into your hand."

The five kings were found huddling in a cave and were slain. Their bodies hung until the evening. That day the LORD wrought a great victory for Israel and Gibeon.

The people of Gibeon never forgot what Joshua did for them that day. It was a sacrificial forced march through the night by Joshua and his men that had saved them. They had done nothing to deserve the salvation he brought them other than simply to ask for it.

Chapter Twenty-Eight

"So Joshua took the whole land, according to all that
the LORD said unto Moses; and Joshua gave it for
an inheritance unto Israel according to their
divisions by their tribes. And the land rested from
war."

Joshua 11:23

1372 B.C.: Shechem

Nearly fifty years had passed since
Joshua's long day at Gibeon. All the
land had been conquered and more
great battles won. At the waters of Merom, Joshua
faced an even greater alliance than that of
Adonizedek. With horses and chariots the enemy
came as the sand of the sea and by the strength and
courage of the LORD the children of Israel defeated
them.

They had a kingdom now, and they had some
land of their own. Though they had all the land
promised to Moses, there still remained within that
land pockets of Canaanite resistance which over time

needed to be driven out. The Abrahamic land grant still remained unfulfilled.

Time had proven a few things since this journey began, one being that when fathers failed to pass down their faith it simply wouldn't be passed down on its own. Though Ishmael and Esau loved the LORD in their latter days, they failed to pass it down, and their children became the enemies of God and Israel.

Another thing taught was the timeless rule of eventual human collapse. Except for the mercy and constant intervention of God, Israel would have fallen prey to the wickedness of false gods, followed by their own destruction.

Time showed us that sin always has consequences. Moses wasn't able to enter the land because of sin. The children of Lot, the Moabites and the Ammonites, became two of Israel's deadliest foes. Hundreds of thousands of Canaanites died because of their debauchery and refusal to obey the LORD and return the holy ground to the sons of Jacob.

Caleb wanted that mountain and with Othniel's help, he took it. Afterwards Caleb let Othniel marry his daughter. The young man continually grew in the LORD and eventually became the first judge of Israel.

Deep within the heart of the earth, in Paradise, Joseph was happy to hear that his bones were finally buried in the Promised Land. Moses and Abraham met together and had a wonderful time telling stories and discussing what they believed was yet to come.

Up in Heaven, Michael and Gabriel argued about who within the tribe of Judah carried the line. Neither one of them considered Rahab the harlot to be anywhere in the picture.

In spite of all the wonderful things that had happened, the seed had not yet arrived. There was still work to be done.

Joshua was old and feeble as he stood before the congregation. His hands trembled, his voice quivered a little. Yet within his heart remained the strength and ferocity of a lion. All the eyes of Heaven and Paradise were fixed upon the great soldier of faith as he addressed the people one last time.

"I am an old man now, old and well stricken in age. I can't see as well I used to, but I hope you can see what the LORD has done for you. The LORD your God has fought for you, O Israel. Behold, this day I am going the way of all the earth: and ye know in all your hearts and in all your souls, that not one thing hath failed of all the good things which the

LORD your God spake concerning you; all are come to pass unto you, and not one thing hath failed thereof.

"Now I've divided out the land for all of you according to your tribes and your inheritance."

His eyes narrowed and his voice grew stronger now. "Now you need to finish what we've started! Drive out the inhabitants and possess what the LORD has given you. Only be ye very courageous to keep that which is written in the Law of Moses, and the LORD will drive them out for you.

"Hearken to me, O sons of Israel! If you join with the remnants of this land the LORD is going to curse you! They will be snares and traps before you."

Joshua spoke powerfully, but he began to pause more and more. His mind went back to Egypt and his time as a slave, working under fear and bondage. He remembered the deliverance at the Red Sea and God's provision of manna. The time God honored his word at the crossing of the Jordan River. The victories of Canaan.

He also remembered the horrible task that was given him: destroy everyone that breathed in the land of Canaan. God had sent an angel to warn the people, but they had chosen to stay. They hardened their hearts to fight against Israel. They were wicked and vile people who worshipped false gods and sacrificed their babies to the fires of Moloch. Even their children were riddled with disease as a result of their parent's wanton fornication with strange flesh. The wickedness of the Ammonites was very much full and God had sent Joshua to exact his justice.

But that didn't make it easier. Joshua wasn't raised a killer; he was a potter within Egypt. He didn't like fighting, yet he had slain thousands by his own hand. He had seen the blessings of living a clean life; he not only had seen the curse of living wickedly before the LORD, he had been God's sword of judgment.

It was thoughts like this that rattled around in his mind as the old warhorse struggled, though only occasionally, to convey his message. He spoke of how obeying the command of the LORD wouldn't be enough; they needed to do it out of love for him. He spoke of Abraham and the promises that remained.

And yet more thoughts clouded his mind. Joshua and his wife had not lived the most cherished of lives, but it was the life that God had given them. A young bride she had married him as a slave in Egypt. She followed him as he wandered through the desert. She faced living in tents her whole life with sand, heat, scorpions, lizards, and constant thirst. She spent many nights alone while her husband fought and fought and fought, always wondering, always dreading that the day would come when he wouldn't return home. In spite of the life Joshua had lived and the life that his wife had suffered, he knew the next words he spoke were absolutely true.

"As for me and my house, we will serve the LORD!"

There was no need to confer with his wife; he knew she was a warrior of the faith as much as he was a bearer of the sword. His wife stood behind him as he obeyed the LORD.

"Now listen and listen well. Fear the LORD and put away your idols. You can't serve the gods of this land and the LORD at the same time!"

Joshua heard various people shout about how they would follow the LORD.

"You can't follow him!" Joshua responded. "You can't follow him and hold onto those cursed idols! When are you people ever going to understand that you can't mix this world's ways with God's ways?

"You are soldiers of the LORD; you can't blush to speak his name or fear to own his cause! You can't ally yourself with the enemy and expect to be a friend of God!

"Don't think to be carried to the skies on flowery beds of ease while others fought to win the prize and came through bloody seas! Is this vile world a friend to grace to help you unto God? Are there no foes left to fight?

"Hearken to me, O Israel, until he comes and calls us home, we're called to be soldiers. I've been a soldier all my life, and I expect to die a soldier.

"I wouldn't have it any other way. If I had to do it all over again, I wouldn't have it any other way."

He who dwelt in the high and holy place, with him also that is of a contrite and humble spirit, was moved at the words of Joshua. All of Heaven sensed it and the host of angels snapped to attention as the warrior continued to speak.

While Joshua finished up his speech, the eyes of him that inhabiteth eternity looked forward to another day. He saw a man in a dimly lit jail cell kick a rat off his foot while he wrote a letter. He had the scars of forty stripes save one on his back and bore in his body the marks of the Lord Jesus.

"You're about to die," a Roman soldier said to him. "What do you think of that?"

"I wouldn't have it any other way," he replied. "If I had to do it all again, I wouldn't have it any other way."

Further forward the eyes of the LORD looked and they stopped again. They stopped at a man who could have had nearly everything the most powerful organization on earth had to offer. Instead of a red cap, he chose a wooden stake and the merciless flames that licked his body. His last words were, "Jesus, Jesus."

Again his eyes moved forward to a time in which men of God put down blades of iron, and in their place lifted up spiritual swords and with shields of faith fought for an invisible kingdom. They, like Joshua, fought all through the dark of night until the bitter end. The soldiers of the cross faced foes and obstacles of every kind; and at the very end if you would ask them, they'd all say the same thing:

"I wouldn't have it any other way. If I had to do it all over again, I wouldn't have it any other way."

END OF BOOK ONE

Epilogue

Two Hundred Years Later, Somewhere in Israel.

"How ya been, Mike?" Satan sneered as he lighted down next to the archangel.

"I've been watching over his kingdom, helping his people defeat their enemies. There's nothing I'd rather do."

"Yeah, well, you certainly do stay busy with that. Don't you ever get tired of the rotating door? One moment they're free, the next they're not, and on and on it goes. Doesn't the constant rinse and repeat wear you out?"

"It would be nice if he came right now. That way I wouldn't have to have these conversations with you."

Satan laughed. "By the way, while you've been busy running in circles, have you had a chance to look at my kingdom?"

"You mean other than smiting your servants every chance I get?"

"Yes, other than that. I bet you haven't noticed I've given my Baalite religion a facelift?"

Michael was weary of the conversation, but his curiosity overcame him. "Okay, I'll bite."

"Why yes, I'm actually very proud of what Wormwood has done. We've already laid the plans to keep Baalism going right up to the end. I believe it will be a very effective tool. In fact, I think I'll just use Baalism to imitate whatever your boss does in the future."

Michael laughed. "That's ridiculous! I have never heard anything that absurd. They couldn't be any further apart than they are."

"Oh really?" Satan gleamed, "Are you certain? Why, Mike old buddy, by the time my kingdom comes to its fullness, it'll have a branch for every bird to land on. I'm really going to enjoy my time down here."

"Okay, what are you up to?"

"Just look at Dan."

"They're backslidden and they've been that way for awhile. What's your point?"

Satan smiled. "Well, my friend, did you happen to notice how they arrived there? Did you notice that they have a priest to help the people worship statues and images? Isn't that just the perfect mixture to make everyone happy? A little bit of what you have to offer and a little bit of what I have. Shouldn't that please everyone?"

Before Michael could respond the devil went on.

"And did you happen to notice that the priest took a vow of poverty when he joined up with Dan? How holy, how pious, how unbelievably convincing! Do you like the way they all call him father?"

Satan began to laugh. "Imagine that! The best part of all of this is that they don't know any better! They think they're serving your God!

"And I've just begun! I plan on imitating everything. By the time I'm done my people are going to be killing your people, and the whole time they're going to be thinking they're doing God a service.

He stepped close and put his face within inches of Michael's. "And then when my kingdom is in full swing and my anointed one is where I want him, we'll rip off the mask and go right back to the drink offerings of blood and the golden calf . . .

". . . right to where we were under Nimrod."

Am I a Soldier of the Cross
Isaac Watts, 1674-1748

1. Am I a soldier of the cross,
a follower of the Lamb,
and shall I fear to own his cause,
or blush to speak his name?

2. Must I be carried to the skies
on flowery beds of ease,
while others fought to win the prize,
and sailed through bloody seas?

3. Are there no foes for me to face?
Must I not stem the flood?
Is this vile world a friend to grace,
to help me on to God?

4. Sure I must fight, if I would reign;
increase my courage, Lord.
I'll bear the toil, endure the pain,
supported by thy word.

5. Thy saints in all this glorious war
shall conquer though they die;
they see the triumph from afar,
by faith they bring it nigh.

6. When that illustrious day shall rise,
and all thy armies shine
in robes of victory through the skies,
the glory shall be thine.

Other books by
Rick and Melissa Schworer

15 Simple Steps
Losing Your Salvation

Faith and Finance:
Peace With or Without
Prosperity

Roadmap Through Revelation